CW00539365

the dandelion diary

Maysen Jar
Series

WALL STREET JOURNAL BESTSELLING AUTHOR
DEVNEY PERRY

1001 DARK NIGHTS
PRESS

THE DANDELION DIARY

Copyright © 2023 by Devney Perry

All rights reserved.

ISBN: 979-8-88542-050-1

No part of this book may be reproduced, distributed or transmitted in any form or by any means, including photocopying, recording or other electronic or mechanical methods, without the prior written permission of the author except in the case of brief quotations in a book review.

This is a work of fiction. Names, characters, places and incidents are the product of the author's imagination or are used fictitiously. Any resemblance to actual events, locales or persons, living or dead, is coincidental.

Cover: Sarah @ OkayCreations.

other titles

Maysen Jar Series

The Birthday List

Letters to Molly

The Dandelion Diary

The Edens Series

Indigo Ridge

Juniper Hill

Garnet Flats

Jasper Vale

Crimson River

Sable Peak

Clifton Forge Series

Steel King

Riven Knight

Stone Princess

Noble Prince

Fallen Jester

Tin Queen

Lark Cove Series

Tattered

Timid

A Little Too Wild

Ivy

Coach

Holiday Brothers Series

The Naughty, The Nice and The Nanny

Three Bells, Two Bows and One Brother's Best Friend

A Partridge and a Pregnancy

contents

prologue

Dear Diary,

My dad needs a girlfriend, and I've already picked her out. Miss Adler would be perfect for him, right? She's super pretty. She has the best smile and gives the best hugs. And she's the most amazing teacher in the world. Dad is my hero, but I can tell he's lonely. He tries to hide it from me, but sometimes at night, when he thinks I'm asleep, I'll sneak downstairs and find him sitting on the couch, staring at nothing. He's never had a girlfriend, not since the divorce. Mom messed him up. She's good at that. He's smart and funny, but he doesn't laugh enough. I've seen other moms at school check him out so I guess he's handsome. (Eww) And he makes up the best nicknames. He calls me Dandelion. I bet he'd give Miss Adler an awesome nickname too. They're perfect for each other. I just know it. Now I only have to show them I'm right.

Wish me luck.
Katy

one
Jeff

"Dandelion," I called from the base of the stairs. "We have to go."

"Almost ready!" Katy yelled.

That was the fifth time she'd promised she was almost ready in the past thirty minutes. "Sixty seconds."

"Coming!" Footsteps pounded overhead as she ran from the bathroom to her bedroom.

We were going to be late. I hated being late. But if there was a female in this world I'd wait for, it was Katy.

Abandoning the stairs, I went to the coat rack in the entryway, taking down my black Carhartt and shrugging it on. Then I patted my pockets, making sure I had my gloves and beanie. "Thirty seconds."

"I'm hurrying, Daddy!" Her voice had that panicked shriek I'd heard every morning this week.

It was probably her hair. Again. Every day this week, she'd come down upset about her hair.

When I'd asked what was wrong, when I'd pressed for specifics, I'd just gotten muttered responses. Maybe it was the style. Maybe the cut. I didn't have a damn clue. She just *hated her hair*.

I dragged a hand through my own thick, brown strands, wishing I'd taken the time to learn hair before she'd become a preteen.

There were dads who knew how to braid or make fancy twists or wield a curling iron. If I could turn back the clock to when she was three, when it was just me to tame her wispy dark-blond strands, I wouldn't have just combed it out and sent her on her way to daycare. I should have learned how to do the braids.

Did twelve-year-old girls wear braids? Even if the answer was yes, we didn't have time.

"Fifteen sec—"

"I'm ready." Katy's boots pounded on the steps as she came flying down the staircase. Tucked under her arm was the diary I'd given her for her birthday. I'd picked it because of the dandelion on the cover, the white puff with seeds flying.

"Coat and gloves." I took the backpack from her shoulder when she hit the entryway, holding it as she snagged her magenta coat from a hook. "Grab a hat too."

She stilled, her eyes widening. One arm was in her coat, the other frozen midair. "Do I need a hat?"

"Um . . ." *Damn.* This was a trap, wasn't it? Yes, she needed a hat. It was freezing outside. But if I told her to wear a hat, would she think it was because of her hair? "You don't need a hat."

Her shoulders sagged. "I hate my hair."

"I love your hair." I reached out and tugged at one of the long, fine strands.

"Hailee called it mousy brown."

"Okay," I drawled. "Is that bad?"

"That's an ugly color."

"It's not an ugly color."

Katy's hair fell nearly to her waist. It was fine and soft and as straight as wheat stalks, nearly the same shade too.

"You have to say that." She rolled her eyes. "You're my dad."

"It's not an ugly color."

"Yes, it is." She huffed and pulled on her coat, then stuffed her diary into her backpack.

Wasn't twelve too early for shit like this? The drama with other girls. The self-conscious thoughts about a hair color. "I thought Hailee was your friend."

"She is."

"But she called your hair ugly."

"No, she just said it was mousy brown."

So where the hell did she derive ugly? We didn't have time for that question, so I reached for the door, holding it open for her to step outside first. A blast of icy cold swept into the house before I closed the door and shuffled Katy down the sidewalk to my truck parked against the curb.

I'd scraped the Silverado's windows already and started it ten minutes ago so the cab would warm up. But parking outside was not ideal, especially in these cold months.

"I really need to get the garage cleared out," I muttered, more to myself than my daughter.

"You say that every day."

"Do I?" I opened the passenger door for her, waiting until she was inside before I handed over her backpack.

"Yeah, Dad. You do."

"Want to do it for me?"

She shook her head. "No way."

"Even for an allowance boost?"

"Have you even seen the garage?"

"Touché." I groaned and closed her door, rounding the hood for the driver's side.

The garage was a clusterfuck. My own fault.

I'd spent the past five years remodeling the interior of the house. The detached garage had been my staging area for tools and supplies. There was enough sawdust on the floor to fill a fifty-pound flour sack. There were wood scraps and power tools scattered from wall to wall.

The remodeling was done. Just last month, I'd finished the dining room, replacing the old carpet with the same white oak hardwood flooring I'd put throughout the rest of the house. But I had yet to haul the nasty carpet roll to the dump, so it was shoved against the garage's overhead door.

By the time I cleaned everything out, spring would be here. Maybe next winter, I wouldn't have to scrape ice from the truck's windshield.

"Can I dye my hair?" Katy asked as I pulled away from the curb.

"No." Hard no. "You're twelve."

"Then when can I dye it?"

"When you're thirty. The same time you can date."

"Dad." She gave me a flat look.

I was getting that look a lot these days. It came with this newfound sass. My baby girl, the light of my life, was growing up too fast. "Tell me what you don't like about your hair. Not what Hailee said. You. What don't *you* like?"

She drew in a long breath, her frame slumping as she exhaled. "I don't know."

"Do you want to cut it? Get a different style?"

Katy lifted a shoulder. "Not really. I like it long."

"So it's just the color you don't like."

"I guess."

I reached across the cab to put my hand on her shoulder.

"You're too young to dye your hair, Dandelion. Your hair is beautiful. I love how it flies behind you whenever you run. I love how it shines like strands of gold when the sun hits it just right. And I hope you can put Hailee's comment aside and realize just how beautiful you are. Mousy isn't an ugly color, baby. It's just a color."

Her chin fell, nearly to her chest, as she stared at her lap. "What does homely mean?"

Homely? "What the fuck?"

Katy gasped, her face whipping to mine. "Don't cuss."

"Sorry." That would be a dollar in the cuss jar tonight. "Where did you hear homely?"

"Hailee."

Time to reevaluate our friendship with Hailee. "Did she call you homely?"

"Not me. She said it about Samantha."

Yep, Hailee needed to go. Of Katy's friends, Samantha was the one I actually liked best. "Samantha is not homely."

The girl just had a long, skinny face and a prominent nose sprinkled with freckles. But she was cute. Not nearly as pretty as Katy, but certainly not homely.

"What does it mean?"

"It's not nice," I told her. *Fucking Hailee.* A twelve-year-old mean girl. Was this what Katy had to look forward to for the rest of middle school? "We're done listening to Hailee."

"But—"

"Done, Katy." I shook my head. "Your hair is beautiful. It's dark blond. And Samantha is a nice and lovely girl, okay?"

She sighed. "Okay."

"Hey." I tugged on her ear.

"What?"

"Who loves you the most?"

"You," she whispered.

"Trust me?"

Katy nodded.

"Today, spend less time with Hailee. See how you feel at the end of the day." I had a hunch she'd be in a happy mood when I came to pick her up this afternoon. And my girl was smart. She'd put it together. "Can you do that for me?"

"Yeah."

"Thank you."

She glanced over, giving me a tiny smile. "Can you do something for me?"

"Depends. What is it?"

"Guess."

"Hmm." I turned down the road that would lead us to the school. "Ice cream for dinner?"

"Nope."

"Good. It's too cold for that." We'd had snow on the ground in Bozeman for months and it showed no signs of melting anytime soon. This was the coldest winter in Montana I could remember.

The indigo mountains in the distance stood proud and beautiful, their caps dusted in white. The local skiers were overjoyed that we'd been getting daily fresh powder. But I was ready for some sunshine and green grass.

"Next guess?" Katy asked.

"The dog."

Katy had been begging for a puppy for months, ever since Hailee—the new bane of my existence—had gotten a golden retriever for Christmas.

It wasn't that I was entirely opposed to the idea of a dog, but spring and summer were my busiest times of year. My life was about to go from hectic to chaotic. I didn't need a puppy keeping me up all night. I didn't need another ball to juggle when I already had ten in the air.

"Just think about it." She clasped her hands beneath her chin. "Pretty please?"

"I'll think about it."

That seemed to be enough to pacify Katy. She relaxed in her seat, eyes aimed on the road as we drove to school.

I managed to make up a couple minutes, but that was where my luck stopped. A block from school, we hit the drop-off line, twice as long as normal. "Shit."

"Don't cuss," Katy scolded.

"Shoot."

She rolled her eyes. "With all the money you put in the cuss jar, I can just buy my own puppy."

Hell, she could buy two puppies.

"We're going to be late, huh?" she asked.

"We're cutting it close today."

But the line moved quicker than I'd expected, and as the SUV ahead of us pulled away from the curb, I stopped and leaned across the cab to kiss Katy's cheek. "Have a good day. See you after school."

"Bye, Daddy." She hopped out, slinging her backpack over her shoulders, then waved before racing off to join a group of girls standing beside the flagpole.

Hailee was in the mix. I shot her a glare, then headed across town for work.

Alcott Landscaping was located on the outskirts of Bozeman, past the expensive neighborhoods where the homes were four or five times larger than my simple three-bedroom cottage. Turning off the paved highway, I rolled down the gravel lane toward headquarters.

My boss, Hans Barton, had owned Alcott for the past ten years. When he'd decided to relocate our shop and headquarters to this acreage for more equipment and supply storage space, he'd asked me to make this property a showcase.

Bordered by a wooden, split-rail fence, the driveway veered past open fields currently buried beneath snow. But in the spring, they'd be a lush green and teeming with wild-flowers.

The office building was simple with brown and gray barn-wood siding. Its plethora of windows offered clients and staff a view of the surrounding gardens and pathways. The show-case. From fountains to native grasses to flower beds packed with colorful blooms in the spring and summer, it had taken me years to finish.

When I'd been hired on at Alcott Landscaping all those years ago, I hadn't planned on it becoming my career. All I'd cared about was a decent paycheck to fund my court battle with Rosalie.

The owner at the time had been Finn Alcott. He'd hired me for hard labor, and damn, I had worked hard. This job had become my escape. Any chance to make an extra dollar, I'd raised my hand.

Still, even working my ass off, it had been almost impossible to keep up on bills plus pay my smarmy lawyer. But Finn hadn't just been my boss. He'd tossed me a life raft when I'd been drowning. When he'd learned of my custody battle with Rosalie, he'd given me the name of his own attorney, a man who'd agreed to represent me pro bono.

Thanks to them both, I hadn't lost my daughter.

Not long after my divorce, Finn had sold Alcott Land-scaping to Hans. And while I hadn't seen Finn in years, he'd always have a special place in my heart. The same was true for Hans.

In the past ten years, I'd come to admire and respect Hans. He'd once had a landscaping company in California but had sold it to retire in Montana. Anyone who knew Hans knew why his retirement hadn't lasted. The man couldn't sit still. So he'd approached Finn and bought Alcott.

Hans had kept the company name—smart, because of its reputation. And he'd retained the employees who'd wanted to stay, including me.

When I'd outgrown laying sod and plowing snow, the foreman had given me other jobs, like irrigation and operating the larger equipment. After two seasons, I'd decided it was time to get some education.

The weeks when Katy had been with Rosalie, I'd filled my time with studying. And after a few years, I'd earned my degree in environmental horticulture with a landscape design emphasis from Montana State.

From lawn mower to Alcott's head designer and general manager, I rolled into the office some days and still couldn't believe the titles on my business card.

The parking lot was half full this morning, mostly office staff. The outdoor crew was light at the moment and would be until spring. There were a couple of trucks outside the massive steel shop building this morning, each fitted with a plow blade on front. We'd beefed up the winter employees in the past few years to offer snow removal to more clients around town, but still, it was quiet.

That quiet would be short-lived. In two months, once the May projects started, the yard would be chaos from sunrise to sunset.

Parking in my usual space, I headed inside. The scent of donuts and coffee greeted me as I pushed through the door.

"Morning," I called.

Korbyn, my assistant, poked his head out of the break room, his cheeks bulging and his hand clasped around a maple bar.

"Save one for me," I said.

He grinned, still chewing, and saluted me with the donut as I headed down the hallway for my office.

At six three, Korbyn and I were the same height, but I had at least fifty pounds of muscle to fill out my frame. Hans called him String Bean—not to Korbyn's face. Hans didn't spend much time in the office these days and had struggled to remember the newer employees. That, and he was horrible with names—it had taken him nearly three years to call me Jeff instead of Big Guy. Rather than try to remember the constantly changing faces, he mostly avoided the crews these days.

Not that he needed to interact with them much. Not when I was running Alcott.

"Morning, Jeff," Rachel said as I passed her office.

"Good morning." I dipped my chin, then ducked into my office across the hall from hers.

She gave me enough time to hang up my coat and shake the mouse on my computer before she swept through my door, her arms overloaded with papers and an iPad. "I need help."

"You got it. Just let me grab a cup of—"

Korbyn strode in carrying a steaming mug and a maple bar on a plate.

"Coffee," I said. "Thanks."

"You got it, Jeff. Anything else?"

I picked up the cup, blowing on the black liquid before taking a careful sip. "No, thanks."

Korbyn winked at Rachel, the two clearly having planned this ambush for the moment I got here. Smart. If you didn't catch me in the morning, chances were, I'd get busy and the day would run away from me.

"Ready?" Rachel asked.

"Am I?"

She adjusted her thick-framed, tortoise-shell glasses. "Every single one of my bids is falling apart."

"They were fine yesterday."

"A lot has changed since yesterday."

I took another sip of coffee, then leaned my forearms on the desk. "All right. Then let's put them back together."

Two hours later, she returned to her own office, projects back on track. And I opened my inbox to a slew of new emails. When I finally looked away from the monitor's screen, my stomach was growling.

"Lunch." I scanned the office, then groaned. I'd been so worried about getting Katy out the door, I'd forgotten my lunch in the fridge at home. So I picked up my phone, about to order a sandwich when it vibrated in my hand, the school's name flashing on the screen.

"Hello," I answered, standing from my chair and ready to grab my coat if Katy was sick.

"Mr. Dawson?"

"Yes."

"Hi, this is Della Adler. Katy's English teacher."

Miss Adler. Katy's favorite. "Hi. Is everything okay?"

"Well, not exactly. Normally, I'd hand disciplinary matters over to Vice Principal Jones, but in Katy's case, since this is the first time we've had an incident, I wanted to talk with you about it directly."

"Hold up." I plucked my coat from its hook. "Did you say disciplinary matters?"

"Um. Yes. Would you be able to come to the school? I've got Katy in my classroom for lunch."

"On my way." I ended the call and strode from my office. "Korbyn, I've got to take off. Would you clear my calendar this afternoon?"

"On it," he said as I breezed past his desk in the lobby and pushed out into the cold.

Disciplinary incident? What the hell was going on? Katy had never, ever gotten in trouble with a teacher. Not once. This had to be a misunderstanding, right? Or maybe another kid had caused some trouble and tried to blame it on Katy?

I tore across town to the middle school, parking in the guest lot. Children laughed at recess as I hustled inside, checking in at the office and getting directions to Miss Adler's classroom.

My footsteps were too loud in the hallway, echoing off the lockers, but the bell rang, drowning them out. Doors opened and kids flooded from classrooms, some carrying lunch bags and all with coats. The noise was intense as they headed in the opposite direction, probably for the cafeteria.

I waded through the sea of little faces, making my way to a classroom with its door propped open. My only visits inside the middle school had been to the gymnasium for an awards assembly and a Christmas choir concert.

Rosalie had insisted on attending the parent-teacher night at the beginning of the school year and subsequent conferences, so I hadn't met any of Katy's teachers. Maybe that had been a mistake.

Was this about Hailee? If that little shit had done something to get Katy in trouble . . .

My hands balled into fists as I strode into the classroom.

The woman seated behind the desk made my steps falter.

Damn. That was Katy's teacher?

Her dark hair was pinned into a messy updo. She wore a pair of baggy tan overalls with a fitted white shirt beneath and a plaid scarf around her throat. A stack of rainbow beaded bracelets decorated her left wrist.

Katy was always talking about Miss Adler's clothes. How

she dressed like a cool kid, not a stuffy teacher. In my head, I'd pictured an older woman, not a woman in her late twenties.

And I certainly hadn't pictured a woman so, well . . . *damn*. She was beautiful.

She turned toward the door, her caramel eyes taking me in as she stood and extended a hand. "Mr. Dawson."

"Jeff," I corrected, taking her delicate hand in mine. "Nice to meet you, Miss Adler."

"Likewise. And it's Della." She shook my hand, then gestured toward the desks.

Where my beautiful daughter was seated in the front row. "Hi, Daddy."

"Dandelion." I crossed the room, propping on the edge of the desk beside hers. "What's going on?"

Katy's gaze flicked to Miss Adler.

Mine followed.

She'd returned to her chair, her arms crossed. Her posture screamed disapproval, but her expression was gentle as she looked at my daughter. "This is the third day in a row where Katy has caused a disruption in my classroom."

"Katy." I pointed to her head, looking between the two of them. "This Katy?"

Della nodded.

The Katy in question pulled her lips in, like she was fighting a smile. Wait. Did she think this was funny?

"What kind of disruption?" I asked.

"She has been cursing in class."

"Cursing?" No way. Not my kid.

"She's used a few colorful words, mostly under her breath," Della said. "But loud enough that other students have overheard and either snickered or brought it to my attention. Today's was the *f* word."

The *f* word. My daughter had said the *f* word? I blinked, then turned to Katy.

Guilt was etched on her face, but she still looked like she was about to laugh.

"What the fuck?"

two
Della

Now I knew where Katy had picked up the language.

"Daddy." Her eyes widened.

"Shit—shoot. Sorry." Jeff ran a hand over his mouth, like he was trying to erase the slips. "Katy, wait in the hallway."

The second he pointed to the doorway, she slid out of her chair and picked up the backpack resting at her feet. There was an odd look on her face that I couldn't quite place. It wasn't a smile, not exactly. But it was a smile, sort of.

It was as baffling as her cussing. Katy was not the girl to cause a scene. Up until this week, she'd always been a perfect student.

She was about to scamper away, but before she could leave, Jeff stopped her. "Wait."

Katy looked up at him and they shared an unspoken conversation. Her shoulders drooped. That non-smile smile vanished. Then she turned to me, apology and sincerity written all over her cute face. "I'm very sorry, Miss Adler. I promise it won't happen again."

"Thank you, Katy."

She walked out of the room, rounding the corner. Then came the thud of her backpack hitting the floor.

Jeff stood, taking a step toward my desk. Wow, he was tall. Long legs. Narrow waist. That Carhartt coat only accentuated the width of his broad shoulders. "I'm sorry. For her language. And especially mine."

"Don't worry about it." I quite enjoyed a well-placed *fuck*. Just not from sixth graders.

"Thanks for calling me, Miss Adler."

"Della," I corrected. Most parents called me by my first name. "And you're welcome. This is totally out of character for her. Is there something going on at home?"

"She hates her hair." He sighed. "It feels too early for her to hate her hair, but what do I know? At her age, all I cared about was sports."

"Middle school is hard." So was high school, for boys and girls both. "But there's no big change or something that might be causing this behavior?"

"Not that I know of. Unless something is happening at her mother's house. But she hasn't been there for a few weeks. My ex wasn't feeling well last week so Katy stayed with me."

"Maybe she misses her mom then?"

Jeff huffed. Not a yes or a no. Just a huff before he dipped his chin. "I'll talk to her. Make sure this doesn't happen again."

"I'd appreciate that."

With a nod, he walked across my classroom to join his daughter in the hallway.

My eyes tracked his every step, taking in his wide frame and the strength of his thighs as they flexed beneath those tan carpenter pants. There was a surety to his steps, not a swagger but a confident stride. And *hot damn*, he had arguably the most perfect ass I'd ever seen.

Curved and muscled and begging to be sq—

Whoa whoa whoa. No, Della. My gaze slammed onto the linoleum floor. What was I doing?

Never in my career had I fantasized about a parent. Never, ever. And here I was drooling over Jeff's ass? What was wrong with me?

Maybe because he'd taken me by surprise. I just hadn't expected him to be so handsome.

From his dark hair to the straight nose and full lips. He had a rugged, stubbled jaw and a gravelly voice.

No excuses. He was Katy's father and there were boundaries. So I stood from my chair, shaking my head, hoping to pop my thoughts back into appropriate territory. Okay, so Jeff was hot. So what? That didn't change the fact that he was entirely off-limits.

Maybe I should have called her mother. Only Katy had told me her mom was sick and this week, she was with her dad. I'd expected to meet, well . . . a regular dad. Not a man who could be a ranch-wear model.

I crept toward the door, drawn closer by that masculine timbre as he spoke to Katy.

Lingering by the door frame, I peered into the hall. Katy leaned against a row of navy lockers.

Jeff had dropped to a knee in front of her so they could talk at eye level. "Okay, Dandelion. What's going on?"

Dandelion. He called her Dandelion. My hand pressed to my heart. That nickname was as adorable now as it had been when I'd learned it minutes ago.

"It just slipped out." Katy shrugged. "You cuss all the time."

"Yeah. But I'm an adult," he said. "You know there are words you're not allowed to say until you're old enough.

Besides, aren't you busting me every five minutes, making me fill the cuss jar whenever I slip up?"

"Sorry, Daddy."

He put his hand on her cheek. "This is not okay."

"I know."

Katy's behavior this week had been a complete shock. She was normally so sweet. Innocent. Smart and diligent with her studies. Not that I'd ever admit it, but she was my favorite student, which was why I hadn't sent this straight to the vice principal. I didn't want this on her official record. If it happened again, we'd have to have a different conversation, but hopefully it wouldn't come to that.

Jeff's thumb stroked her cheek before he ran his palm over her hair. "Never again, okay?"

"Okay," she whispered.

The gentleness and attention he gave her was as adorable as her nickname. And surprising. Maybe that was why I couldn't tear my eyes away from Jeff. After what Katy's mother had told me, the mental picture I'd created for Jeff seemed very different than reality.

Rosalie and I had met at the beginning of the year when she'd brought Katy to orientation. We'd visited for a few minutes, and Rosalie had seemed kind. Appreciative. But when Katy had gone out to test the combination of her locker, Rosalie had warned me that Jeff wouldn't be involved. What was the word she'd used? *Deadbeat.*

He didn't seem like a deadbeat. Not in the slightest.

"What's your punishment?" he asked her.

Katy tapped a finger to her chin. "Dishes for, um . . . five days."

He narrowed his eyes. "It's pretty bad when a teacher calls a dad."

"A week of dishes?"

Jeff shook his head. "A week of dishes and all the laundry. Mine included."

"Eww." She scrunched up her nose. "Your stuff is so smelly."

"Maybe after a week of dealing with my stinky socks, you'll remember to watch that mouth in school, huh?"

Katy heaved a sigh. "Okay."

The corner of his mouth turned up. Also sexy.

Apparently everything he did was hot.

He crooked his finger, and she flew into his chest, wrapping her arms around his neck.

Yep, that was attractive too.

He held her like she was his entire world, loved more than she'd ever know.

As Jeff let her go and stood, holding out his hand for hers, I stepped into the hallway. "See you tomorrow, Katy."

She gave me a finger wave. "Bye, Miss Adler."

"Thanks," Jeff said.

"Bye." I lingered beside the lockers as they started down the hallway, watching as he slowed to let his daughter set the pace.

Don't check him out. Don't check him out.

That ass was like a magnet, drawing my focus. It really was perfect.

A throat cleared.

I jumped, whirling. Luka hovered beside my shoulder. "H-hi."

He smirked. "Admiring the view?"

"Stop." I elbowed him in the ribs, hoping he wouldn't notice my flaming cheeks. "They're cute together."

"How's your day going?"

"Good, actually." After I'd called Jeff, I'd prepared for the worst. Most parent meetings were a foolproof way to ruin an otherwise nice day. But that meeting had been a breeze. "How is your day?"

Luka clapped his hands together, rubbing them as he gave me an evil grin. "Pop quiz for my class after lunch."

"You get far too much enjoyment from torturing your students."

"Probably." He winked, the same devilish wink he'd been giving me since college.

Was it flirting? I'd been trying to figure that out for a decade.

Luka dragged a hand through his dark blond hair. No matter how often he combed it with his fingers, it always seemed to lie down in the perfect place.

He'd been born and raised in Montana but would pass as a professional surfer without question. He had a tall, strong frame ripped with muscle. The tousled hairstyle. The cocky smirk. The sparkling blue eyes. All he was missing at the moment was a tan.

But he practically lived outside in the summers. Sooner or later, he'd have that tan. Maybe this year, I wouldn't drool over him shirtless.

"See you at home?" he asked.

I nodded. "I'm swinging by the store after work. Need anything?"

"Condoms."

"Luka." I poked his rib, giving him a scowl as he laughed.

Was he joking about the condoms? I couldn't tell.

"Enjoy the rest of your day," he said. "Highly recommend working in a pop quiz."

"I pity your students."

His chuckle filled the hallway as he walked away, his long strides lazy and confident.

Luka had a swagger. And for years, it had made me swoon.

But as Jeff slowly meandered with his daughter, I couldn't decide which stride I liked best. My arrogant roommate and friend. Or the dad who shortened his steps so his daughter didn't have to rush hers.

I let myself take one last glance at Jeff's muscled behind before I sighed and retreated to my classroom for the remainder of my day. Unlike Luka, I preferred smiles on my students' faces over looks of terror. I lived for the engaging discussions and peeks inside their blossoming minds.

Middle schoolers always had a way of surprising me. They rarely said what I expected and they didn't miss much. This was the age when sarcasm bloomed.

Katy Dawson had a dry humor. Why did I have a feeling she'd learned it from her dad?

The remainder of my classes went smoothly. When the last bell chorused through the hallways, it was followed by the explosion of kids racing for their lockers. I waited until the noise subsided, the kids streaming outside for buses and activities, then did a few final tasks before grabbing my coat and heading outside myself.

My trip to the grocery store was efficient. I breezed through the aisles, snagging every item on my list—refusing to go anywhere near the condoms.

Luka and I were . . . complicated. For years, more than I was willing to admit, I'd held out hope that one day he'd see me. Want me.

Those hopes had faded lately. Once upon a time, my feelings for Luka had been as vibrant as a rainbow, iridescent strokes in a blue sky. Now they were hazy, like a fog had rolled in and cast everything in gray.

So now he was just my friend. A coworker. A roommate.

At twenty-eight, living with a roommate wasn't ideal. But Bozeman real estate was ridiculously expensive, and I was on a teacher's salary. Some of the other single teachers lived in neighboring towns where rent was cheaper, but I didn't want a thirty- or forty-minute commute on icy winter roads. Plus, I loved Bozeman. It was trendy and charming.

So two years ago, when I'd gotten sick of living in a college neighborhood, dealing with keg parties and midnight antics, Luka and I had moved in together.

Our two-bedroom house was in downtown Bozeman, in a neighborhood full of young families and single retirees. Most people assumed Luka and I were a couple.

I liked that. Or I had, once.

The neighbors who did think we were together had clearly missed the unending stream of women that flowed in and out of Luka's bedroom. Either he was just that good about sneaking his hookups in and out of the door, or they thought he was a pig cheating on me.

Maybe both.

Sooner rather than later, I needed to move. With every passing day, I itched to change my address. This living arrangement was only supposed to be temporary until I saved up some cash for a down payment on my own place. Splitting bills with Luka, the cheap rent, meant that with every paycheck, my savings account was growing.

But my balance just wasn't enough. Not yet.

I parked my mint-green Jeep Wrangler on the street outside the house, then I looped my grocery bags over my forearms and made my way inside, stomping the snow off my shoes in the entryway.

"Della?" Luka called. "That you?"

"Who else would it be?" I asked, shuffling to the kitchen, plopping bags on the counter.

He rounded the corner from his bedroom dressed in a pair of gray sweats and a Montana State University hoodie. "How was the store?"

"Fine." I unbagged a bunch of bananas, setting them on the counter while he put a carton of eggs and a bag of shredded cheese in the refrigerator.

We worked in tandem, emptying the bags. Two people who'd lived with each other for years. Two people who'd known each other long enough to feel entirely comfortable in our bubble.

Maybe too comfortable. Too stagnant.

"No condoms?" he asked, peering in the last plastic sack.

I rolled my eyes. "You're exhausting."

He chuckled. "But you love me anyway."

"Love?" Yes. In the past. But now? "Maybe. Maybe not."

He smiled wider. It had become this little game of mine, letting my inner thoughts come loose, just to see if he realized they weren't as sarcastic as I made them out to be.

"How much do I owe you?" he asked.

I plucked the receipt from my purse and handed it over.

He did the quick math, then went to the whiteboard we'd hung on the wall, adding forty-seven dollars and sixteen cents to his column. As part of our living arrangement, we'd decided to split utilities and food equally.

Like we were a couple. That whiteboard had become a constant reminder of what we shared. And what we didn't.

But we weren't a couple. He'd made that clear.

"Okay, I'm going to change and then—" Before I could offer to make dinner, the front door opened.

"Luka?" A female voice drifted from the entryway.

My eyes shot to his.

He just shrugged and went to meet his guest.

No wonder he'd called out for me. He'd been expecting someone else.

A leggy blond with striking blue eyes stood at his side when he returned to the kitchen.

"Oh, uh, hi." She gave me a finger wave with the hand not linked with Luka's. God, she was young. Probably a senior in college.

"Hi." Why hadn't I grabbed a bottle of wine at the store?

Luka didn't bother introducing her, if he even remembered her name. He just jerked his chin to the hallway, his silent cue that they were disappearing to his bedroom.

My stomach knotted as they vanished. The dull click of his door echoed down the hall, followed by her muted giggle.

They always giggled.

When would this stop bothering me? When was I going to get over him?

Another giggle.

"Not today," I muttered, sweeping my purse from the counter. Then I walked to the door, slamming it too hard before I stomped to the Jeep.

So much for dinner at home. At least I had a good alternative.

On nights when Luka and his sexcapades drove me from the house, I retreated to my favorite café in Bozeman.

The Maysen Jar.

My junior year at Montana State, when I'd been buried beneath a mountain of credits, I'd struggled to find a place to study. The library had lost its appeal when I'd found Luka and another girl from the education program making out on the third floor. So I'd decided to break free from campus and find a place of my own.

Three coffee shops later, I'd been about to suffer at the

library, but then I'd stumbled upon The Maysen Jar. I'd been coming back ever since.

After parking the Jeep, I made my way inside the restaurant, breathing in the scent of cinnamon, sugar and vanilla.

The building itself had once been a mechanic's garage, until Poppy Goodman—Maysen, until she'd married her husband—took the place and transformed it into a charming café.

The red brick walls stretched to the ceiling, the ductwork exposed to give it an industrial flair. The original garage doors had been replaced with a row of tall black-paned windows. My shoes, wet from the snow outside, squeaked on the hickory herringbone wood floor as I made my way down the center aisle, passing black tables and chairs filled with happy customers.

"Hey, Della." Poppy waved from behind the counter at the back of the café. Her smile was contagious. An instant mood lift.

"Hi." I pulled out a wooden stool, taking a seat beside her daughter, leaning over my former student's shoulder to see what she was studying. Math. I nudged her elbow with mine, earning a smile as bright as her mother's.

MacKenna plucked out her earbuds and stretched out her arm for a sideways hug. "Hi, Miss Adler."

"Hey. Heard you had a pop quiz in math today."

"Yeah." She groaned, tucking a lock of loose, brown curls behind her ear. "Mr. Hollister."

Luka wasn't exactly beloved by his students. Not that he seemed to care. If he did, well . . . he hadn't shared those feelings with me. Maybe he preferred to confide in the blond during their postcoital pillow talk.

I fought a lip curl, focusing on MacKenna. "Hanging with your mom tonight?"

"Yeah. Dad took Brady to basketball."

Poppy's husband, Cole, was a cop in Bozeman. Their son Brady was still in fifth grade, but I was keeping my fingers crossed that I'd have him in my class next year.

MacKenna had been my favorite student last year. Like Katy Dawson was this year. And I had a hunch Brady would be next.

"Can I get you anything, Della?" Poppy asked.

"Surprise me."

"I was hoping you'd say that. I tried something tonight and MacKenna agreed to be my test subject. But I always love more opinions."

"You know I'll always be a test subject." It wasn't the first time she'd let me eat one of her experiments. They were always delicious and always ended up on the menu.

"They're in the back oven. I'll check if it's ready." Poppy held up a finger, then turned and disappeared through the swinging door that led to the kitchen, her sleek red ponytail swishing across her back.

"Okay, so what are we working on?" I leaned my forearms on the counter, inching closer to MacKenna to see what home-work she was tackling.

The two of us powered through not only her math assign-ments from Luka but also her social studies homework and her latest grammar worksheet from her seventh-grade English teacher—her most boring teacher, MacKenna's words, not mine.

While we worked, we ate Poppy's latest creation, a vegetable lasagna with a creamy white sauce that was, as expected, perfection. Time passed in a blur and when I finally left them to close the restaurant for the evening, I felt lighter. Only that lightness was short-lived. With every block closer to home, unease twisted my stomach.

Luka's date would be gone, right? He rarely let them spend the night.

Regardless, it shouldn't be like this. A woman shouldn't dread going home because her roommate was screwing his latest conquest.

I parked in my usual spot in front of the house. Since it was Luka's house, he parked in the garage. My Jeep was alone on the street, and fingers crossed, that meant his guest was gone. Bracing for giggles or the sound of his headboard smacking the wall, I inched through the front door.

Luka lounged on the living room couch, phone in hand, dressed in the same sweats from earlier. His hair was damp.

He liked to shower immediately after sex.

"Didn't mean to chase you from the house." He gave me an apologetic smile. "She left."

"It's fine." I waved it off. Was it fine?

Maybe. Maybe not.

A year ago, I would have retreated to my room to wallow. Five years ago, there would have been tears. But tonight, I just didn't have the energy. So I made my way to the couch, sinking into the buttery leather and pulling a throw across my lap before snagging the remote.

"I was going to use that blanket," he said.

"Snooze, you lose, Hollister."

He chuckled as I turned on the television. "Nothing girly."

"We're watching *The Parent Trap*. The original with Hayley Mills."

Luka hated this movie. But like his pop quizzes, it was my form of torture. He felt guilty for the blond, so he'd stay on this couch and watch until the credits rolled. And tomorrow morning, he'd go out early and scrape the Jeep's windshield of ice for me. He'd be up early to work out at the gym, then he'd come back and make us both lunches.

Was that why I hadn't moved yet? His considerate touches always seemed to reel me in. That, and maybe I was scared to spend my nights on a couch alone.

None of it mattered. Not a little bit. Because I was not a woman in Luka's fantasies. He'd starred in my fantasies for a decade, yet I'd barely been a side character in his.

Dreams of Luka came less and less these days. Instead, I dreamed of a faceless man who cherished me wholly. A man who was considerate. Sweet. Maybe a man who was just as tall. Just as handsome.

And while I was pulling items from the dream-guy menu, I wanted him to have an ass like Jeff Dawson's.

three
Jeff

The house was too quiet.

There were no footsteps thudding upstairs as Katy raced through the hallway. No K-pop blaring from her bedroom. No frustrated groans about her hair.

I fucking hated shared custody.

Katy was at her mother's this week. We'd been doing this week-on, week-off thing for a decade. Wasn't it supposed to get easier?

Years ago, when I'd been in school earning my degree, these were the weeks I'd bury my nose in books and block out her absence with my studies. During peak landscaping season, I'd lose myself in mountains of work, avoiding the house from six in the morning until eight at night. And the hours I was home, I'd be swamped with remodeling projects.

Except I'd been too productive. Too efficient. The house was done, and I doubted the work I had on my desk would take until four this afternoon.

Did I need a new hobby? I'd already worked out this morning in the small home gym I'd built for myself in the basement. Maybe I should get Katy that puppy. At least I'd have another living being in the house. Or maybe tonight, I'd stop slacking and get started on organizing the garage.

I cast a longing glance up the staircase as I headed for the front door, then I dug out my phone to send Katy a text.

love you dandelion

With my coat on, I paused in the entryway, waiting for her reply. She'd become the grammar police this year, so I purposefully ignored commas and capitalization just to get her reaction.

Was that Della Adler's influence? Probably.

In the past week, Della had popped into my mind more times than I wanted to admit. I kept picturing her chocolate hair. Those caramel eyes. The sweet mouth.

A jolt of lust shot straight to my groin, making my cock twitch. *Fuck.* That had happened more times than I wanted to admit too.

When was the last time I'd had this reaction to a woman? Years. Not since three winters ago, when I'd had a no-strings fling with a former client. Both of us were divorced and hadn't wanted any type of commitment beyond sex.

At least, that was what we'd agreed upon. But that hadn't stopped her from coming over four months later and asking for more.

I didn't have more.

My dating history was, well . . . nonexistent. Not once in my life had I taken a woman to dinner and a movie. Not even in high school. Not even Rosalie.

I'd just never met a woman I'd wanted to date. To chase. And these days, limiting complication was the goal.

The last thing I needed was another ex-wife. The occasional one-night stand and an orgasm or two was all I had to offer. Even then, the women hadn't been addictive. The moment I'd crawled out of bed, it was over. So what the hell was it about Della?

I'd spoken to her for a whole ten minutes. Yet something about her was . . . different. Lasting. Maybe because Katy talked about her all the time. Because it felt like I'd known her before we'd ever met.

For months, Della had infused our conversations. When I asked Katy about school, *Miss Adler* was usually part of her reply. She was an undercurrent in our text threads and the grammar lashings doled out by a twelve-year-old.

Whatever my interest was with Della, it would pass, right? Hell, I doubted I'd ever see the woman again. So I shook her out of my head, made a quick adjustment to my dick, then checked my phone again—still no reply from Katy.

"Huh." Not normal. Katy was always quick to reply in the mornings. But maybe she'd gotten distracted, so I tucked my phone away and headed outside.

I was the first to arrive at the office, but Korbyn walked in thirty minutes later, knocking on my office door with a yellow sticky note between his fingers.

"Morning, Jeff."

"Morning." I saluted him with my steaming coffee mug. "What's up?"

He waved the note. "Hans called. Wants you to call him back."

"All right. Thanks." I picked up my desk phone and punched in Hans's number.

"Jeff?" He answered on the first ring.

"Hey."

"I'm just rolling in. Be there in a sec."

" 'Kay." I hung up, then snagged my phone, checking for a text from Katy. Still nothing.

We texted all the time. When she was with Rosalie, she

had to ride the bus to and from school, and in that forty-minute commute, she'd blow up my phone with fifty texts because while hers were all grammatically correct, she never included two sentences in the same message.

You okay?

I stared at the screen, waiting for those three dots to appear in reply to my message, but it stayed blank. So I turned on the ringer so it would chime whenever she replied before setting it aside, just as Hans appeared in my office's doorway.

He was dressed in a ratty flannel shirt this morning, the sleeves rolled up his forearms and the hem untucked. One knee of his jeans was damp, like he'd dropped it in the snow outside. His white hair was cut short, but his matching mustache was a creature of its own, bushy and thick.

"Good morning." I gave him the same coffee-mug salute I'd given Korbyn.

"Hi." He shuffled inside and closed the door. *Well, shit.* Hans never closed the door, even when he was having a private discussion.

"Am I going to like this meeting?" I asked.

"Yes?"

"Why did that sound like a question?"

Hans chuckled and took a seat, kicking up an ankle over his knee. "I'll cut to it. I'm retiring."

The tension ebbed from my shoulders. His retirement was nothing to worry about because the man wouldn't retire. This was the third time in five years he'd come in here to announce his retirement. "Sure."

"I'm serious this time." He pointed at my face. "After this season, I'm retired."

"Okay." I didn't buy it for a damn minute.

My hunch? The season would come and go, and instead

of setting a retirement date, he'd spend the winter talking about employees and budgets and special projects.

"You don't believe me," he said.

"Nope." I took a sip of coffee.

"Then maybe this will convince you. I'd like to sell you Alcott."

My hand froze midair, mug included. That was new.

During the previous discussions, he hadn't mentioned a long-term plan for the company. Part of why I'd never believed he'd actually retire.

"Believe me now?" He smirked, the ends of his mustache lifting.

"Back up." I set my mug aside before I dropped it, then leaned my elbows on the desk. "You want to sell me Alcott?"

"Yep."

In my wildest dreams, I wouldn't have expected this. Sure, I enjoyed working for Hans. I loved this job. But owning the business? That wasn't something I'd even let myself hope for.

"I can't afford it." The words burned as they came off my tongue, but it was the truth. "Thank you. I'm honored that you'd think of me. I just . . . I don't have that kind of money."

Alcott Landscaping was worth millions.

I had a mortgage and a lackluster savings account.

"You don't need that kind of money," Hans said. "I'm not searching for a lump payment. I'm looking for retirement income."

Huh? My brain was still stuck on the fact that he'd even thought of me as his successor. "I'm not following."

"We'll draw up a contract. Basically, treat this like you're taking out a loan but instead of from a bank, from me. You run Alcott. It's your business. And every year, you pay me a certain amount."

"That sounds . . ." *Too good to be true.*

Hans must have read my mind because he gave me a gentle smile. "I don't have kids. No one to pass this down to. The idea of selling it to a stranger, having to watch someone else run this place, makes my skin crawl. This morning, I said as much to Mary. She smacked me across the head with the newspaper and told me, 'Then don't sell it to a stranger, dummy.'"

I'd always loved Hans's wife. Still, it seemed too out of the blue. Was something wrong? Was there a health concern I didn't know about? "Where is all this coming from?"

He shrugged. "I'm ready. Finally. Mary and I want to travel. It will be an adjustment, but usually I'm excited this time of year. Anxious for the season to get started. This year? I'm dreading it."

"We can handle everything. If you want to travel, travel. You don't have to sell Alcott to do that."

"No, I know myself well enough that if I don't cut myself off, I won't walk away. It's time." There was a weary note in his voice. He sounded tired. Serious.

"Why me?"

"That's a dumb question. And the wrong question." He scoffed. "Why not you?"

Why not me?

"Good?" Hans asked, not really wanting an answer. He smacked his palms on his knees and stood, moving for the door. "I'll have my lawyer draw something up. Are there any donuts in the break room today?"

Another question I didn't get the chance to answer before he opened the door and disappeared down the hallway, like he hadn't just changed my whole goddamn life.

Own Alcott? Fuck yeah, I wanted to own Alcott. But could

I do it? There was a big difference between working for a business and running it. Was I up for it?

Why not me?

"Holy shit." I swept up my phone, wishing I could talk to Katy. She was only twelve, but that girl was my best friend. When something good happened, she was the first to get the news.

Except when I called her number, expecting to hear her voice combatting the noisy chaos from the bus, it went unanswered.

"What the hell?" Where was my daughter?

Katy never forgot her phone. Never. And not just because she was a responsible kid. From the time she was eight, I'd made sure she not only had a phone but also a watch. She might live with her mother part-time, but I wanted full-time access to my child. Day or night.

That phone, her watch, were essential to my peace of mind.

Fear raced through my veins as I typed out another text.

call or text Katy I'm starting to worry

I waited, willing the phone to ring, but it stayed quiet.

She was fine. Even as my heart raced, my palms getting clammy, in my head I knew she'd probably just left her phone at home. She hadn't forgotten it before, but for a kid, it was bound to happen. Maybe the watch hadn't charged last night.

And if something bad had happened, Rosalie would have called me. Confidence in my ex was severely lacking, but when it came to emergencies, she didn't have the stomach to gut them out. She'd call.

So I did my best to work for a few hours, but worrying was as constant a distraction as my silent phone.

It was nearly lunchtime when it rang. I flew for it, twisting so fast in my chair that I knocked over my coffee cup—thankfully empty.

The school's name lit up the screen.

"Hello?" I answered, already out of my chair.

Fuck. I knew it. Something was wrong. I should have acted sooner. Should have checked in with Rosalie. Should have called the school.

"Hi, Mr. Dawson."

"Miss Adler." Later, I'd analyze why I recognized her melodic voice. "Is Katy okay?"

"She's, um . . . she's having a bad day. Any chance you could get away from work for a quick visit?"

"On my way." I strode from the office, not slowing to tell Korbyn where I was going. He could assume I was on my way to lunch. Then I raced across town, breaking every speed limit posted until I was at the school and jogging down its hallways.

Similar to my visit last week, Della's classroom was empty save for Katy in her desk, arms folded on the surface. Instead of being in her own chair, Della was crouched beside my daughter, her hand trailing up and down Katy's spine.

"Hey, Dandelion."

Katy's head flew up, her face streaked with tears.

My heart cracked. Did all dads hurt when they saw their kids cry?

"What happened?" I picked her up from the desk, hoisting her up from beneath her arms, and hauled her into my chest.

There'd come a day when I couldn't pick her up. Thank fuck, it wasn't today.

Katy's arms wrapped around my neck, holding tight, as she pressed her face into the crook of my neck.

Outside, kids were playing on the playground. Their

shouts and laughs carried through the tall windows. I just held my daughter closer. "Are you hurt?"

Katy shook her head.

A sliver of panic faded. "Are you in trouble?" *Please, don't be more cussing.*

This time it was Della who shook her head, giving me a kind smile as she stood. "She started crying in class today. I pulled her aside and gave her some space, but she's had a hard time stopping."

Damn. I bent, setting Katy on her feet. Then I pulled her arms away because she wouldn't let go before dropping to a knee so we could talk face-to-face. "Lay it on me, shortie."

That earned me a slight smile.

Katy hated any endearment or nickname besides Dandelion.

She sucked in a shaky breath, then blew it out as her shoulders slumped. "Mom took my phone and my watch so I couldn't even call you today and she did it because she knows I was going to text you on the bus and she's mad at me because she promised she'd take me to this restaurant and then she changed her mind and I got upset and she said I was acting like a brat even though she was the one who broke her promise."

"Wow." I pulled in my lips to hide a smile. That was a load to unpack. Mostly, I was just really glad she was okay.

Over Katy's shoulder, Della ducked her chin, fighting a laugh.

"That's a lot," I said.

Katy nodded, wiping beneath her eyes. "Mom's the brat."

"Hey, now. Don't say that." I'd used plenty worse when it came to Rosalie, but I didn't want Katy to walk that road.

"It's true." The scowl on her face was adorable. I'd take that over the tears anytime.

"We'll get this all sorted out, okay?"

"Okay." Katy sniffled, wiping her nose with her sleeve.

Rosalie had no right to take that phone from Katy, not without checking with me first. I'd given Katy that phone and watch. I floated the bill. She should have asked me first. A conversation I'd have with my ex soon.

The restaurant thing we'd tackle next week. I had a hunch the place she wanted to go was called Jar something. She'd mentioned it last weekend on the drive to Rosalie's place— too quickly for me to recall the name and too late for me to actually take Katy there for dinner. She'd also mentioned something about a girl in seventh grade and her mom who owned it or something.

Whatever. I'd get the scoop tonight. After Rosalie returned Katy's phone.

"Better?" I asked. "Think you can make it through the rest of the day?"

She nodded. "Yeah."

"That's my girl." I tucked a lock of her hair behind an ear. "I've missed you this week."

"Missed you too."

Della cleared her throat. "Katy, if you hurry, I bet you can still eat a quick lunch and have five minutes on the playground."

"Okay." She flashed her teacher a smile, then flew into my arms, hugging my neck so tight I couldn't breathe. Then she was gone, hair streaming behind her as she ran out of the classroom.

I sighed, letting my heart finally sink back into my chest.

Della wasn't in overalls today. Instead, she was in a black dress with puffy sleeves. The boots she wore only came to the ankle, giving me the perfect view of toned legs encased in green and black checkered tights.

Of course she had great legs. Tonight I'd probably imagine them wrapped around my waist. Not exactly thoughts I needed to be having about my daughter's teacher.

I shoved to my feet, giving her a nod. "Appreciate the call, Miss Adler."

"Della," she corrected, just like she had last week. Somehow, calling her Della felt too intimate. It erased that imaginary boundary between us. But that didn't stop it from rolling off my tongue.

"Della." Pretty name for a pretty woman.

She cocked her head, studying me. Her eyebrows came together with the slightest crease.

"What?"

"Nothing." She waved it off and smiled. "I adore Katy. She's so sweet and a wonderful student."

"She adores you too. And whatever you're teaching her is working. She loves to pick apart my texts and correct me when I don't write them properly."

Della stood a little taller. "Really? I sort of love that."

"So do I."

"You call her Dandelion? That's a unique nickname. Where did it come from?"

"When she was little, she used to follow me around the yard whenever I mowed. She'd pick every dandelion flower she could find and bring me these bouquets. She said it was her favorite flower, so I started calling her Dandelion."

"It fits."

"I think so." I grinned, taking in the sparkle in her eyes. That color was mesmerizing. Not just caramel like I'd thought last week, but there were a few flecks of shining copper too.

I opened my mouth, about to tell her she had beautiful eyes, but caught myself. "I, uh . . . I'll let you get back to work."

"Yeah, I um . . ." The color rose in her cheeks as she glanced to her desk. "Me too. Bye, Mr. Dawson."

"Jeff." It was my turn for corrections.

She dipped her chin. "Jeff."

Even the way she said my name sounded pretty.

But pretty wasn't the right word. She was captivating. Breathtaking. Stunning. Surprising. Tempting.

And Katy's teacher.

It was time for me to put some distance between us before I said something stupid and made it awkward.

With a wave, I turned and strode for the door, about to escape into the hallway when I nearly collided with another man. I shifted out of the way in time to avoid a crash in the threshold. "Sorry."

"No problem." The guy was about my height and size. He looked me up and down, then strode into Della's classroom.

I glanced over my shoulder, just in time to see her eyes dart up from my ass.

Damn. Was she interested? Because that would be fucking awesome.

For Della Adler, I'd learn how to date. Unless there were other rules at play? Could teachers and parents get together?

"Hey." The man, another teacher probably, walked straight to Della, stopping close. Too close. He put his hands on her shoulders, a move not normal for coworkers.

Ah. Of course she'd have a man in her life.

The twinge of envy was hard enough to send me out the door and down the hall. After passing a row of lockers, I glanced back, hoping to see him leave her room, but the hallway stayed empty.

Why was I even jealous? She was a beauty, sure. But I didn't date for a reason.

That reason was on the playground at the moment.

It was better this way. Maybe knowing Della was taken would stop me from thinking about her legs tonight. Probably not, but maybe.

I picked up my pace, wasting no time on my way back to work. Then I spent the rest of my day answering questions and reviewing design plans, anything to keep my head from wandering.

Hans had offered me the chance of a lifetime this morning. Was I twisted up about Alcott? No. I was stuck on Della. On the way I'd caught her checking out my ass even though she was tangled up with someone else.

Maybe that should have made me mad, but damn it, I couldn't shake the jealousy. By the time I left the office, the last place I wanted to go was home. It was too quiet. So I did a quick internet search and found that restaurant Katy had told me about.

The Maysen Jar.

That seemed like a great place to kill an hour.

The café was an old building that someone had fixed up, small enough to be cozy but big enough you weren't sitting on top of other patrons. The minute I stepped inside, the smell of fresh bread and apple pie hit my nose.

My stomach rumbled. It was comfortable. Welcoming. Like I was stepping into a friend's house, not a restaurant.

All but two of the tables were full. My boots thudded on the wood floor as I made my way toward the counter at the back lined with stools. Normally, a single stool would suit me just fine. But tonight, sitting alone felt too miserable.

Katy's puppy was starting to sound more and more appealing, and I did not need a damn dog. Instead, I'd sit at a table. Pretend I was waiting on someone else. So I ordered—mac 'n' cheese and a salad, both served in jars—and took my food to one of the free spaces, settling in with my phone.

I'd been putting off the call to Rosalie all afternoon, mostly because talking to her gave me a headache. But I pulled up her number anyway, bracing for whatever attitude would greet me on the other end of the line. Before I could hit send, a throat cleared at the base of my table.

And there she was, the woman who'd invaded my thoughts. Every time I saw her she just kept getting more beautiful. How was that possible?

"Hi, Jeff."

Still liked how she said my name. Still liked those legs in her tights. Still liked the pretty colors in her eyes.

Not a chance I'd be able to stop thinking about my daughter's teacher tonight. *Damn.* "Hey, Della."

four

Della

There was one empty table at The Maysen Jar.

The table situated right beside Jeff's.

"I, um . . . nice to see you again." My hands smoothed down the skirt of my dress, then tucked twin locks of hair behind each ear. My fingers flexed, hanging in midair for a moment, searching for their next target—the puff on one of my sleeves.

Fidgeting. That was a new trick. *Oh God.* I hadn't felt this nervous around a man in years. Not since those early days in college when I'd met Luka. But I'd known him for so long, the jitters that came with my crush had faded.

Was that what this was? A crush?

If only I'd spotted him earlier, I could have snuck out the restaurant's door before he'd seen me. But there was no way I could leave now, not without seeming rude. Besides, I was starving and I'd already ordered my food.

So here I was, fidgeting.

I cast a look toward the front counter and the row of empty stools. The loner's section. I'd wanted a table tonight, not just because I'd brought along papers to grade and wanted space to sprawl, but because I hadn't wanted to be the only person at the counter.

So I slid into a chair at that empty table, sitting beside Jeff with a two-foot gap between our shoulders, and set down my Diet Coke. Poppy wasn't here tonight, but the waitress was making my dinner and had promised to bring it over once it was out of the oven.

"How was the rest of your day?" Jeff asked.

"Good. Uneventful. I don't know if my students will ever learn how to use commas correctly, but it's become my personal challenge to get at least one kid to know the rules. Katy might just be that kid." Rambling. I didn't ramble. *Get it together, Della.*

I risked a glance Jeff's way, taking in his profile. There was a small bump on the bridge of his nose. He had a strong chin. A soft pout. And that jaw . . .

Chiseled. Granite.

Yep, definitely a crush. On my student's father. This was so, *so* bad.

"I wish I could offer to help Katy with the comma situation," he said. "But I'm rather helpless when it comes to them myself. I'd do more damage than good. Math on the other hand, math I can handle."

Why was that attractive? What was up with me and guys who liked math?

Jeff's gaze caught mine for a brief moment before we each faced forward again.

My cheeks flamed, a mix between infatuation and the awkwardness of sitting side by side. We were like two teenage kids at a theater trying not to look at each other but so painfully aware of the other that concentrating on anything else was impossible.

"Here you go, Della." The waitress came to my rescue, placing a tray on my table. "Can I get you anything else?"

"No, thanks." I gave her a kind smile, then busied myself with unrolling my silverware and draping the napkin across my lap.

"First-name basis here, huh?" Jeff asked.

I shrugged. "I come here a lot."

"This is my first time. It's good. Very good. After Katy's outburst today, I figured why not try it out. Then I'll bring her here next week."

"I saw her this afternoon on the playground. She was laughing with a group of her little friends. Like this morning's tears never happened."

His eyes softened, something that happened a lot where his daughter was concerned. "Appreciate you helping her. And calling me."

"Of course." I dug my spoon into my chicken pot pie, letting the steam escape the top crust.

The restaurant's front door opened, a couple stepping inside. They glanced around, both searching for an empty table.

"Mind if we share a table?" Jeff asked. "Free one up?"

"Not at all." This would be better, right? At least we could face each other.

Jeff shifted his dinner, moving it to my table before he took the chair opposite mine.

Our gazes locked. That heat in my cheeks spread.

Nope, this was worse. Much, much worse. Now it felt like we were on a date.

Whatever. We'd survive a quick meal and then I'd go home. The papers I'd grade at the dining room table. If I was lucky, Luka would be gone when I got there. He'd mentioned possibly going to the gym.

I took a bite, still too hot but I let it scald my tongue anyway.

Jeff opened his mouth like he was going to say something, but then must have decided against it because he took a bite of his mac 'n' cheese.

"I eat alone a lot," I blurted as he chewed. "I think I'm out of practice sharing a table with someone."

He swallowed, nodding. "Same. My only dinner companion these days is Katy. And she usually carries the conversation."

"Then we're doomed."

He chuckled. It was a rumbled laugh, one that came from deep in his chest, and sounded almost as nice as the way he spoke my name.

"My roommate is the chatty one at my house. Luka." Apparently, even with a burned tongue, the rambling wasn't going to stop. "He came into the classroom earlier as you were leaving. He teaches math. Katy will probably have him next year. He has an affinity for pop quizzes."

"Noted." Jeff took another bite.

"Luka and I actually went to college together. We've been friends for years and were both lucky to get a job in the Bozeman school district."

Wait. Why the hell was I talking about Luka?

He was part of the reason I'd come here tonight. The last place I wanted to be right now was at home with a Luka who was acting *not* like Luka.

Right as Jeff had been leaving my classroom earlier, Luka had come in and given me a hug. Luka hadn't hugged me in a year. The most affection he showed me was the occasional high five or fist bump.

I'd shrugged him off, not something I'd ever thought I'd

do, but he'd been acting so . . . strange. Guilty. That hug attempt had felt a lot like a farce. A plea for forgiveness.

Luka's blond had come over again last night. Like the time before, he hadn't even bothered with an introduction before whisking her off to his bedroom.

I'd made the mistake of staying home, sequestered in my room, knowing exactly what was happening in his bedroom. Well, not tonight. I'd left before there was even a chance at an encounter.

I dug my spoon into my jar, about to take a bite, but noticed Jeff's jars were empty. While I'd been blathering about Luka, he'd inhaled his food to get the hell away from this table.

Well, it wasn't awkward anymore. We'd skipped to sheer mortification.

"Sorry," I whispered at the same time he said, "I eat fast."

"Pardon?"

Jeff gestured to his empty jars. "I eat fast. My boss told me once there wasn't a limit on the number of times I could chew."

Relief coursed through my veins, the air rushing from my lungs. So he wasn't trying to make a fast escape. He just ate fast. "Oh."

"How long have you been a teacher?" He relaxed deeper in his chair, showing no signs of leaving.

"About five years," I told him, letting my shoulders fall away from where they'd crept toward my ears. "I graduated from MSU when I was twenty-two, but there weren't any positions open at the time so I subbed for a year before I got hired on at the middle school full-time."

Bozeman was one of the fastest growing communities in the country. People flocked to this area of Montana, wanting to escape big-city life but also wanting the comforts that came with a town large enough for a Costco, Target and UberEATS.

With the influx of residents, the city had built three new schools in the past five years. The teacher who'd had my classroom before me had opted to move into the bright, shiny new middle school.

Fine by me. I didn't need bright and shiny.

"Are you from here?" Jeff asked.

"No, I grew up in Prescott. It's a small town about an hour from here. Ever been?"

"I haven't."

"It's worth a trip if you and Katy ever feel like getting out of town. My parents still live there, so I visit fairly often."

"Didn't want to get a job teaching there?" he asked.

"I thought about it, but it's hard to get a job in Prescott. There just aren't enough positions, and the English teacher there is in her thirties with no current plans to retire or move."

Prescott would always be home, though every year I spent in Bozeman, it felt more and more like mine. "What do you do?"

"I'm a landscape designer at Alcott Landscaping."

"Any projects around town that I'd recognize?"

"Maybe. Most of what we do is residential. But you know that park next to the new brewery off Oak?"

My jaw dropped. "You did that?"

"Turned out nice."

Nice? That park was stunning.

Jeff had incorporated these antique elements into the flower beds, from wagon wheels to an old bicycle to a rusted pickup with blooms teeming from its windows and truck bed. The walkways were cobblestone, charming and delightfully imperfect so people couldn't race along the path but were forced to slow down. To take deliberate steps. To appreciate the riot of colorful blooms and their sweet scents.

It was a park where lovers went to stroll. Where old friends met to reconnect.

"You're very talented," I said.

He lifted a shoulder. "Maybe. Mostly, I love my job. Don't think everyone can say that, so I'm grateful."

Hot. And humble.

Yeah, this crush was a bad idea, but who the hell could blame me?

"I have to tell you something," I said. "You're not at all who I expected to meet when you walked into my classroom last week."

His eyebrows knitted together. "What do you mean?"

"Katy's mom, um . . . I just had a different impression about you."

"I see." Understanding dawned and the confusion on his face was replaced with a frown.

Ugh. What was wrong with me? Jeff hadn't raced for the door after he'd eaten but apparently I was trying to sabotage this meal and send him far, far away. Why had I even brought this up?

Earlier today, when Katy had called her mother a brat, Jeff hadn't let it stand. Yet she'd dragged him through the mud to me, a stranger, without hesitation during our first meeting.

I sucked at dinner conversation. "I don't know why I told you that. Sorry."

"Don't be. Appreciate the heads-up. Just wish I could say I was surprised."

"You don't get along?"

He shook his head. "Wish I could say we did."

Jeff seemed so . . . steady. Solid. No hidden agendas. No drama. Granted, we didn't know each other, but I just got this sense from him. Like if a tornado hit this very spot, he'd be the man whose feet never left the ground.

So what had happened with Jeff's ex? Had he cut her loose? Or had he broken her heart? Was revenge the reason she'd called him a deadbeat?

A thousand burning questions popped into my mind but I swallowed them down, concentrating on my meal.

"We got married young," he said.

I put my fork down, giving Jeff my undivided attention.

He stared across the table, his expression so open. Unguarded. I liked that a lot too.

Jeff had the most dazzling hazel eyes. They were a riot of earthy colors from brown to hunter green to flecks of gold and silver.

Katy's eyes. She shared most of her mother's features, from her nose to her mouth to her hair color, but those eyes she'd inherited from Jeff.

Lucky girl.

"Rosalie and I met at a party," he said. "We were young. Drunk. Hooked up and she got pregnant. The way I was raised, you get a girl pregnant, you do your best to make it work. So we got married."

"How old were you?"

"Nineteen."

"Ooof. That is young." At nineteen, I'd been in college, worrying over team projects and if I should get bangs, not a husband and baby.

"Too young," he said. "Most days were . . . hard. But we stayed together for a couple years. I think I was just too stubborn to admit it was a failure."

"You strike me as the type of man who doesn't like that word."

"Not at all." The corner of his mouth turned up. "The divorce was messy. I suspect most are."

I waited for him to explain "messy" but he folded his hands in his lap, no further explanation given. This was his chance to balance the scales, to give me the dirt, but he stayed quiet, letting my imagination run rampant.

"Sorry." He shook his head. "I, uh . . . I shouldn't be saying this. You're Katy's teacher."

So Rosalie could run Jeff down, but he couldn't share his side of the story? Was that because he still loved her? Had he ever loved her?

"You don't have to tell me anything," I said.

"Then why do I want to?" He studied my face, like that question was more for him than me. "Why do I feel like I've known you more than a week?"

"I don't know." But God, I liked it. I liked *him*. More and more with every passing second.

"I don't talk about Rosalie much. To anyone," he said. "It's just easier I guess. To keep it to myself."

"Because of Katy?" Or because he didn't have a lot of confidants. I had a hunch maybe it was both.

Jeff inched forward and dropped his voice. "During the divorce, I mostly referred to her as a vicious bitch. She wanted full custody of Katy, who was only two, and I refused. So she hired a lawyer and started making up stories about how I was a bad father. Said I wasn't ever at home. Said I refused to buy diapers. That sort of bullshit."

"Seriously?" Anyone who spent more than two seconds with Jeff and Katy would see he was a loving and devoted father.

"It was all lies. I wasn't home, because I was working two jobs. And I wouldn't buy Pampers, because they were twice as expensive as Walmart's generic brand."

Hence the "vicious bitch" nickname.

"Took me a bit, but I found a good lawyer. He was a good guy. Knew I was struggling and threw me a bone. Made sure I didn't lose custody of Katy. But through it all, I didn't have a lot of nice things to say about Rosalie. Couple years after the divorce, Rosalie did something that pissed me off. I was ranting to my parents about it and called her a bitch. Katy was four and she repeated it."

I winced. "Oh."

"Decided from that point on, I might not have to like Rosalie, but she's Katy's mom."

So he'd stopping talking badly about her. Meanwhile, Rosalie had jumped at the chance to smear Jeff to her daughter's teacher.

Shame on me for believing her.

"Sorry." He rubbed a hand over his mouth, just like he'd done in my classroom the day we'd met. Like he wanted to erase the words he'd spoken. "You're very easy to talk to. Has anyone said that to you before?"

"A few times." I liked to listen more than talk. I guess that was why people confided in me.

"I can't believe I just told you all of that. Why did I tell you all of that?"

"I'm glad you did," I said. "You're a good dad."

"I am a good dad." A statement. Delivered by a man who'd been called the opposite and who'd worked hard to prove he was worthy.

This crush was going nowhere, was it? *Damn.* I glanced down to my unfinished meal, giving it my attention instead. If I kept staring into Jeff's hazel eyes, I'd be tempted to beg him for an actual date.

And he was totally off-limits.

While Katy was my student, all Jeff could ever be was an

acquaintance. A friend. The district had policies about parent-teacher relationships.

My crush would have to wait. Would he?

Maybe after years of being rejected by Luka, years of pining for that man, I didn't have the guts to ask.

So I ate my dinner, then wiped the corner of my mouth with a napkin. "It was nice bumping into you tonight."

Jeff dipped his chin. "Same. Thanks for keeping me company. And, uh, sorry for the overshare."

"Don't be. And you're welcome." I shifted out of my seat, collecting my belongings and shrugging on my coat while he did the same. Then, instead of heading with him to the front door, I pointed to the counter. "I'm going to grab something to go for my lunch tomorrow."

Jeff lifted a hand. "Good night, Della."

"Bye, Jeff." I turned, refusing to let myself watch him walk out the door. But as I headed for the counter, the waitress checked him out.

Her eyes were glued to Jeff's ass.

So much for her tip on my next order. A surge of possession rushed through my veins strong enough to make me turn.

Broad shoulders. Narrow waist. Long legs. And that glorious behind of honed muscle.

Jeff Dawson was temptation personified.

He pushed through the door, disappearing around the corner to the parking lot while I faced forward, getting a salad for myself. Then I headed home, not sure how to feel. Crestfallen. Giddy. Pathetic.

Had I gotten too complacent? Too stuck in a rut? When was the last time I'd gone out to dinner with a man? I'd all but abandoned dating. Not that Jeff and I had been on a date, but it had been date-ish.

Should I dust off my dating apps? The idea made me grimace as I walked into the house.

"What's that look?" Luka asked from the living room.

"Nothing." I waved it off, taking my food to the fridge.

Just as I closed the door, Luka rounded the corner, leaning a shoulder against the wall. He'd changed out of his work clothes into a pair of black sweats and a zippered hoodie that he'd left undone to reveal the hollow at the base of his throat.

Luka was undeniably handsome. Years ago, I would have fantasized about undoing that zipper the rest of the way.

"You look pretty," he said, his gaze dragging down my dress from work.

I was pretty.

Like Jeff could declare he was a good dad, I was pretty. Sure, some days I had the same insecurities I suspected most women battled, but I felt comfortable in my skin. When I looked in the mirror, I saw more features that I liked than disliked.

So it wasn't the declaration of me being pretty that made me pause. It was the fact that the compliment had come from Luka.

Had he ever called me pretty before? Most of his commentary about me was playful teasing. He'd joke about the rainbow stack of bracelets I wore at least once a week because rainbows made me happy. He'd tease me for the countless shoes stuffed in the hall closet. But a genuine compliment?

I racked my brain but couldn't remember a time when he'd called me pretty.

"Thank you?" It came out as a question.

He grinned. "Want to watch a movie?"

"Sur—" *Actually.* No. "I think I'm going to read."

His smile fell. "Really?"

"Yeah." Really. I didn't feel like a movie with Luka today.

"Night."

Without another word, I slipped past him and went upstairs to my bedroom. After putting on some pajamas, I went to the bathroom to brush my teeth and wash my face. Then I slipped into bed, pulling my Kindle from its charger. But not even one paragraph into the book I'd started last night and my mind wandered.

So I swapped the Kindle for my phone, pulling up Instagram and searching for Alcott Landscaping.

The latest post was of a guy waving from his pickup. On the front of the truck was a plow blade and the caption summarized Alcott's snow removal services. I scrolled through the other winter photos, scanning faces. Searching. No Jeff. Not until the backdrops were snow-free and posted from this past fall.

He was wearing a buffalo-check flannel and a faded black baseball hat, washing his hands in some sort of old-fashioned fountain, seemingly unaware that someone close by had a camera. Jeff's strong jaw was dusted with stubble. Beneath his flannel was an oatmeal Henley, similar to the one he'd been wearing the day we'd met.

I kept scrolling, searching for more. He wasn't shown often. Whoever was in charge of their social media did a great job balancing numerous employees as well as projects, both in progress and completed. But there he was again from last May.

He was smiling in the photo, wearing that same faded hat. His hands were covered in leather gloves as he carried a young sapling toward a hole in the dirt. The muscles in his forearms were flexed. His biceps strained the fabric of his sweaty, white T-shirt. Beneath his dirt-streaked jeans, his thighs were thick, the denim molding around honed muscle.

A pulse bloomed between my legs. My mouth watered.

He was sexy and sweet and—

"Della?" Luka knocked on my door.

I jerked, dropping my phone as I sat up straighter. "Y-yeah?"

"You decent?"

"Come on in." I quickly turned the phone upside down as he turned the doorknob and poked his head inside. "What's up?"

"Just seeing if you're loving your book or if I could change your mind about that movie. But looks like you're not even reading."

"Just catching up on social media." Drooling over my student's father. Same thing.

"Still a no on the movie?"

"I'm going to chill up here."

"All right." He glanced around the room, lingering. What was he doing?

This was my space, and with his suite downstairs, he didn't have a reason to come up here. Until tonight. What was up with him? Had the blond dumped him? That would serve him right, considering he was usually the one to break hearts. Maybe he'd be more careful if he learned how it felt.

Finally, he shifted, pulling the door closed. "Night."

"Good night." I waited until Luka was gone, then sagged against my pillows.

Why did I feel like I'd just been caught doing something bad?

"Because you were," I muttered.

What the hell was I doing? Cyber stalking Katy's father?

God, I was pathetic. This had to stop. So I put my phone away once more.

And spent the rest of the evening trying not to think about Jeff Dawson.

five
Jeff

Sunshine streamed through my truck's windows as I drove down Main, heading toward the office. Alcott's season was officially underway. Over the past two weeks, most of the snow around town had melted, enough that we could start on a few larger projects.

It was muddy as hell, and there were still frozen patches in the ground, but spring had arrived and with it, my days were slammed with client meetings and site visits. It was two thirty, and I'd left the office this morning at seven.

The chime from my phone rang through the cab, Mom's name flashing on the console. "Hey," I answered.

"Jeff? Is that you?"

"Yes." I chuckled. "You called me, Mom."

"I did? Oh." There was a pause, probably because she'd pulled the phone from her ear to check that she had in fact called me. "I thought maybe you'd called me because you haven't called me in sixteen days."

A smile stretched across my mouth. I ended the call, cutting her off, then immediately called her back.

"Did you just hang up on me?" she answered.

"Hey, Mom. Just calling to say hi."

"Funny," she deadpanned. "But you're alive? You're okay?"

"Alive. Okay. Just busy."

She sighed. "I assumed as much, but I wanted to give you a hard time. I miss you."

"I miss you too."

My parents lived about fifteen minutes outside of town in the same house where I'd grown up. Dad was a ranch hand for a man who lived in Boston and only visited once or twice a year. Dad managed the property, maintaining the livestock and various buildings on the land. Mom was a bank teller at a local credit union.

But even though they lived close and she worked in town, we didn't see each other as often as I'd like. They were great about keeping up with Katy, calling or texting her a few times a week. And next week, when her soccer season started, they wouldn't miss a single Saturday game.

"Want to grab a coffee?" I asked. "I was just heading to the office, but I could swing by the bank instead. My treat."

"You're on. I'll only have thirty minutes, so we'll have to be quick. I'll get my stuff and meet you out front."

"Be there in ten." I hung up, then slowed to take a side street and head back the other way.

Maybe we'd go to The Maysen Jar. It wasn't far from Mom's bank. Not that I expected to see Della, but I hadn't been able to get her off my mind.

That dinner we'd shared hadn't been anything special. Not a date, just a run-in. So why couldn't I stop thinking about her? And why the hell had I spilled my guts about Rosalie?

There were only a few people who knew the whole truth about my marriage. Yet telling Della had been as natural as breathing. She'd stared at me with that caramel gaze and it was like the truth I'd kept buried deep for years just poured out.

I didn't want Della believing Rosalie's bullshit. I didn't want her to think I was scum.

Because even though it had just been a run-in, I'd wanted it to be a date. At thirty-one years old, I'd met a woman I wanted to date. To win. Della had left me craving more.

More of that blush to her cheeks. More of those mesmerizing eyes. More of her sweet laugh and dazzling smile.

What were the rules about a parent dating a teacher? My guess . . . it was frowned upon. Or forbidden.

Meaning maybe I wanted more, but I wasn't going to get it.

Probably for the best. My focus right now needed to stay on my daughter and work. Hans hadn't mentioned the sale of Alcott again, but that didn't mean he'd changed his mind. I didn't have time for distractions, and Della Adler was just that.

Maybe I was reading more into this. Maybe I was just lonely. Katy was at Rosalie's this week—I'd get her Sunday. Which meant all I had to do was survive tonight and tomorrow, then my house would feel like home again. I could breathe again.

Katy would be proud when she came to the house Sunday. I'd been working on the garage each night and there was almost enough space to park inside.

My phone rang again as I slowed for a red light. *Rosalie.* I groaned before I answered. "Hi."

"You need to get Katy. I'm sick."

"All right." Years ago, I'd ask what was wrong. Not anymore.

It was probably a headache. Or a stomachache. Or a fever. Or a hangnail.

Before Rosalie, I'd never met a person who was sick so often. I wasn't a doctor or therapist so I had no idea, but it was almost like she enjoyed it. She relished the attention. Maybe that was just me being bitter, but more often than not, she seemed fine.

The short years we'd been married, she'd been sick so often that Katy had needed daycare because Rosalie, who hadn't had a job, *couldn't* watch her. Infant childcare was insanely expensive, but it was either pay or lose my job because I'd have to call in sick to stay home with my daughter.

The illnesses were just as frequent now as they had been at the beginning. But I didn't ask for details. Maybe Rosalie really was sick. Maybe it was a figment of her imagination. Maybe she didn't feel like watching Katy this weekend. Whatever the reason, I didn't give a shit.

The only thing that bothered me was how much time Katy spent at the ER because her mother was notorious for emergencies on her weeks with our child.

"Does she know not to ride the bus?" I asked.

"Yes, I called the school."

"Okay. I'll head over and pick her up," I said. "Do you want me to bring her over tomorrow so you can have your Saturday with her?"

She huffed. "I'm really sick, Jeff. How could you want her to catch this cold?"

I bit back a snide comment. "Then she'll be there next Sunday."

Rosalie waited, like she was expecting me to give her well wishes for a quick recovery.

Instead, all she got was, "Bye."

The moment I ended the call, I called Mom's number.

"Are you here already?" she asked.

"No, change of plan. Rosalie is sick, so I need to get Katy from school."

"Sick." There was an eye roll on the other end of the phone. Mom had spent enough time around Rosalie to know that their definitions of *sick* were vastly different too. "I'd say something nasty about her always uprooting your plans, but I know you prefer it this way."

"Yes, I do."

"It's just . . . what if you had a date or something?"

"Any woman I date would know that Katy comes first."

Maybe that was why I hadn't dated. Because no woman I'd met in years was one I'd want to introduce to Katy.

Until Della. And Katy already adored her.

"Rain check on the coffee?" Mom asked.

"Definitely. Next week."

"Perfect. And don't forget to send me her soccer schedule when you get it from the coach."

"Will do. Love you, Mom."

"Love you too, bud."

I could be fifty years old and she'd always call me bud, just like she had when I was a kid.

By the time I turned around again and drove to the school, nearly all of the buses had left the parking lot, and the last few cars were pulling out of the pickup loop.

Katy was standing on the sidewalk, her backpack bulging and her coat tied around her waist.

Next to her stood Della.

They were both smiling, not paying any attention to the vehicles coming and going. They were entirely engrossed in conversation with each other.

My heart thumped a bit too hard in my chest.

The smile on Katy's face was pure joy. But Della . . .

Damn, but she was pretty when she smiled.

I parked against the curb, shutting off the truck and rounding the hood.

The minute Katy spotted me, she stopped whatever it was she was saying and raced down the sidewalk. "Ready for impact!"

I laughed, bending to catch her as she leapt into my outstretched arms. "Hey, Dandelion."

"Hey, Daddy." She kissed my cheek, then squirmed to be set down.

"How was your day?" I took the backpack off her shoulder, slinging it over mine.

"Good." She looked over her shoulder.

"Hi," Della said, walking our way. Her eyes twinkled under the afternoon sun.

"Hello." I'd been waiting two weeks for the chance to tell her *hello*.

"I thought Mom was coming to get me," Katy said.

"She's sick."

Katy rolled her eyes, then looked up at Della. "She's not really sick."

Even my kid knew Rosalie's symptoms were grossly exaggerated.

"Oh." Della's eyebrows came together as she tried to piece it together. There was more I hadn't told her about the divorce.

"Can we go out to dinner?" Katy asked.

"Sure." I hadn't made it to the store yet. I'd planned that for Sunday morning. "The Maysen Jar?"

Maybe if I planted the seed, Della would just so happen to show up tonight too.

"Or Village Inn Pizza," Katy said.

"So you can play in the arcade."

She clasped her hands beneath her chin. "Please?"

"Okay."

"Yes." She fist-pumped, then looked up at Della. "Want to come, Miss Adler?"

"Oh, uh . . ." Della searched the area around us, like she was afraid someone was listening.

"I'm sure Miss Adler has other plans tonight, Katy," I said. "It's sweet of you to think of me though."

"But you have to eat." Katy, my beautiful daughter, was nothing if not persistent in response to a no. "And everyone loves pizza."

Della just gave her a kind smile. Her hair was down today, the chocolate strands winding around the hood of her thick, cream sweater. She tucked a strand behind an ear.

"Why don't you go get in the truck?" I jerked my chin toward where it was parked. "I'll be right behind you."

"Okay." She sighed. "Bye, Miss Adler."

"Bye, Miss Dawson. Have a great weekend."

"You too." Katy walked to the truck, using the running board to open the back door.

I waited until she was inside before facing Della. "Sorry."

She waved it off. "Don't be."

We stared at each other, both of us not quite sure what to say. The school loomed behind her like a father lurking in the doorway while his teenage daughter was in the car outside with her boyfriend.

Which meant it was time for me to head out. "Have a good weekend, Della."

"You too, Jeff."

I turned, about to disappear into the truck, but stopped. "Six o'clock. If you like pizza."

"Everybody likes pizza."

Was that a yes? This was the problem with never dating. I sucked at it. "Bye."

It took an effort not to look back as I walked to the truck to see if Della was still watching. But when I climbed behind the wheel and checked my mirror, the sidewalk was empty. *Damn.*

"We've got to go to the office for a while," I told Katy. "Then we'll head to dinner."

"Do I have to go to Mom's tonight?"

"Nope."

"Yes." Another fist-pump.

It made my whole day that she wanted to stay with me.

So we went to the office. Katy took out the stash of art supplies in my desk drawer and sketched flowers while I spent a couple hours working—and watching the clock.

Would Della come to dinner tonight? After what she'd told me about her roommate, I realized they weren't a couple. But still, I hadn't asked about the school's rules. Maybe she wanted to share a pizza. Maybe it was too much of a risk.

Still, by the time we left the office at five thirty, I was buzzing with nerves.

We made it to the pizza parlor, getting a booth close enough to the arcade that I could watch Katy play. Then I stared at the door while she raced to a game.

By six, my beer was gone, and Katy had already spent five dollars in quarters. By six thirty, I ordered pizza, trying to hide my disappointment.

Maybe this was a good thing. Hadn't I told myself that earlier? I had other priorities. Besides, maybe she didn't feel the same. Maybe this was entirely one-sided.

I was about to dig out my phone, busy myself with emails, when the door opened. I did a double take.

Della stopped just inside the threshold, her bottom lip

worried between her teeth. She watched a waitress pass by, then smiled at the hostess who asked her a question. With a quick headshake, she turned, like she'd changed her mind.

My breath caught as she moved to push the door open, only to stop herself short.

This time when she turned, her gaze drifted into the restaurant.

To me.

She gulped.

Then she unzipped her coat.

six
Della

I was *so* getting fired.

But did the threat of unemployment keep me from walking to Jeff's table? No. No, it did not.

On the drive to the pizza parlor, I'd rationalized this a hundred different ways. It wasn't a date but an accidental encounter, right? I'd come for pizza and just happened to bump into a student and her father. This was a coincidence—technically, Jeff hadn't even invited me. And it would be rude to ignore them when we were all, inadvertently, at the same restaurant.

He'd simply mentioned his plans tonight, which had happened to match mine—or the plans I'd made after he'd mentioned his.

Oh, hell. This had disaster written all over it.

But still, I kept walking. As long as I kept this crush to myself, no one could assume this was a date.

Secrets worked. Until you told someone.

The school's code of conduct didn't prohibit friendships between teachers and parents. But it did forbid a romantic relationship between a student's parent and his or her teacher while said student was in the teacher's class. A rule designed to ensure there was no preferential treatment.

Meaning that while Katy was in my class, Jeff was totally verboten.

I'd read that policy a hundred times in the past two weeks, just to see if maybe it would change.

It hadn't.

But I could do this. I could have dinner. As long as I didn't cross the line between friendship and romance, this was just . . . pizza.

Everyone loved pizza.

"Hi." Jeff grinned up at me when I reached his table.

"Hey." My voice was too breathy. I sounded like the awkward teenage girls I caught flirting with the scrawny teenage boys beside their lockers. This was *such* a bad idea.

"Want to sit?" Jeff nodded to the booth's bench seat opposite his.

Yes, I wanted to sit. *Should* I sit was an entirely different question. So I stayed standing beside the table, my gaze darting between his empty pint glass, a menu, the parmesan cheese shaker, the red chili flakes and the booth's smooth vinyl, begging for my rear end.

"Della."

I gulped. "This isn't a date."

"This is pizza."

"Exactly." With a sure nod, I shrugged off my coat, laying it in the booth before sliding into my seat. Then I did a quick scan of the restaurant, my frame relaxing when I didn't recognize a single face.

"Here." Jeff slid a glass of ice water across the table. "It's Katy's, but she hasn't touched it yet. She's too busy trying to win a stuffie from the claw grab machine."

Past the booth, in the arcade, Katy was at her game, her

eyes narrowed as she moved the claw with the joystick. "She's adorable."

"I think so too." A smile tugged at his mouth. "So what do you normally do on Friday nights?"

"Clean." And until this very moment, I hadn't realized just how pathetic that sounded.

Wow. I needed to get a freaking life.

Luka was usually gone on Friday nights, off to meet friends or hit up a bar downtown. He used to invite me along, but I'd gotten so tired of watching him pick up women that I'd said no more often than yes, so much so that my invitations had stopped.

Which meant on Fridays, I had the house to myself and would take advantage, cleaning my bedroom and bathroom while I ran a couple loads of laundry.

Boring. Dull.

Time to stop talking about me.

"What about you?" I asked.

"On the Fridays when I have Katy, usually we go out to dinner, then play games at home. When she's with Rosalie, I usually do some cleaning too."

"So we're both boring."

He chuckled. "Instead of calling it boring, how about efficient? We use our free time wisely."

"I like that."

"Me too. I guess we're kindred spirits."

Kindred spirits. I liked that too.

My cheeks flushed as I met his hazel eyes, taking in the swirls of color. The intensity of his gaze only made the blush flame hotter, so I took a drink of the ice water.

This connection between us was so . . . potent. Tangible. It was like a thread stretched between us, a single fiber that kept growing and growing, weaving thicker and tighter, forming a rope.

"How does it feel like I've known you for years?" I whispered.

"I don't know," he murmured. "But I feel the same."

Beneath the table, his shoe brushed mine. A touch so innocent, so simple, but my breath hitched.

"I, um . . ." Why was it so hot in here? I took another drink of water, then steered the conversation away from anything that would get me in trouble. Well, more trouble. "So Rosalie is sick?"

"No." Jeff sighed, his foot staying exactly where it was, pressed against mine. "Yes. Maybe. It's complicated."

From everything he'd told me, everything about his relationship with Rosalie was complicated.

"She is sick a lot," he said. "More often than not, she's got no symptoms. The doctors won't find a thing physically wrong with her. But I think . . . she likes to be sick. Or the illusion of sick. Earn that sympathy. I don't know. When I say it out loud, I sound like an asshole. But it's just my opinion. Maybe there is something wrong with her the doctors can't find."

"Ah."

"It's a sore subject," he said, glancing behind him to make sure Katy was still at her game. "We didn't have good insurance when we were married. After Katy was born, there were bills, but I was on a payment plan, taking care of it. Rosalie would get 'sick'"—he added air quotes—"and rush off to the doctor. Over and over and over again. At one point, she was going weekly. The bills just piled up. Made it feel like I was in quicksand. Just when I thought I'd caught up on payments, she'd sink me a little deeper."

I gave him a sad smile. "I'm sorry."

He opened his mouth, about to say something, then

clamped it shut. "Here I am again, telling you way more than you probably care about."

"I care."

He huffed a dry laugh. "What is it about you that makes it impossible for me to shut up?"

"I don't know." But I liked it. I liked that he confided in me when I doubted he confided in anyone else.

Jeff stared at the table for a long moment. He was debating whether or not to continue, wasn't he?

I hoped he kept talking. His sharing made me feel important. Trusted. Special.

All my life, I'd just wanted a man who'd make me feel special.

"Rosalie didn't want a divorce." He spoke on a low sigh, like he'd accepted this urge to share the whole story. Like the only way he'd be able to stop talking was if I left the booth.

I was not leaving this booth.

"Why didn't she want a divorce?" I asked. Was she still in love with him?

"Security, I think. We weren't happy. We were never in love. Like I told you the other night, I didn't want to admit I'd failed at my marriage. But I realized one day that the misery just wasn't worth it. I didn't want Katy growing up in that environment. So I told Rosalie it was over. She flipped. Flat out told me no. When she realized I wasn't going to change my mind, she got a lawyer."

And that was when he must have started referring to her as a vicious bitch.

"During the divorce, these sicknesses of hers became a nightmare. It was like she was purposefully trying to shove me into bankruptcy."

"Why would she do that?"

"She was angry. Knew the thing I loved most was Katy. So

she tried to take her away. Ruin my chances at shared custody."

"What?" I gasped. "But if she was sick all the time, wouldn't she want help with Katy?"

"If she had full custody, then I was paying higher child support. Enough to where she wouldn't have to get a job."

So she'd tried to take advantage. *Vicious bitch.*

"She racked up a bunch of bills," he said. "We were still married so they were all in my name. Do you know how much it costs to go to the ER with abdominal pain every day for three weeks?"

"Every day for three weeks?" Oh my God. "How much?"

"A fuckton." Jeff dragged a hand over his face. "The hospital ended up garnishing my wages. I was buried in debt. It was awful. But I got lucky. That lawyer I told you I hired? He was a referral from my boss at the time. Took me on pro bono. He was good. Very good. Made sure I didn't lose Katy."

I officially hated his ex-wife. "I'm sorry."

"It all worked out." He checked to make sure Katy wasn't close by again. "Rosalie isn't a bad mom, but she's not a great mom. I have a great mom, so I know the difference. And I can't even say it's Rosalie's fault. It's just what she knows. Her own mother is exactly the same. Always sick. Never working. There's always . . . something. And whatever that something is, it will always take priority over Katy."

Then it was good she could always count on Jeff.

"Thanks for telling me," I said.

"Christ." He shook his head. "You're the first person I've told in years. Ready to run for the door yet?"

"Nope." I patted the bench. "I like this seat."

His eyes softened, a few crinkles forming at the sides. "Glad you came tonight."

"Me too."

This was the riskiest move I'd ever made. Even as a kid, I'd never tried shoplifting a lip gloss or going to a party and lying to my parents about what I was doing. I'd been the good girl, happy to abide by the rules.

With Jeff, the stakes were sky-high. My career was one of the single most important things in my life. But I didn't regret coming tonight. I just couldn't. I liked him too much.

"Miss Adler!" Katy came to a sliding stop beside the table. A wide smile illuminated her face. Beneath her arm was a fuzzy, hot pink duck. "You came!"

"I decided pizza sounded really yummy. Hope you don't mind if I sit with you and your dad."

"No way." She slid into the booth beside me, handing the duck to Jeff. "Look what I won."

"Nice work, Dandelion." He tucked the duck beside him, then handed over a paper kids' menu with a four pack of crayons.

"Thanks. Coloring with crayons is kind of for little kids, but it's all they have here so . . . oh well." She gave me another blinding smile, then went to work. "What's your favorite kind of pizza?"

"The works."

"That's ours too." She colored as she spoke. "Dad is a landscaper. Did you know that?"

"I did, actually." Jeff's gaze was waiting when I looked over. "What's your favorite part about it?"

"Making someone's yard their sanctuary."

Great answer. "I bet you have an amazing yard, don't you?"

"Ha." Katy scoffed. "Dad spends all his time on other people's yards and saves ours for last."

Jeff just shrugged. "She's not wrong."

Something in my chest melted. Maybe it was the way she

teased him. The way he took it. They were so comfortable together. We were all so comfortable, like people who'd been spending Friday nights at Village Inn Pizza for a decade.

Or maybe it was the fact that Jeff gave his energy to others. His daughter. Clients.

There wasn't a self-important bone in his body, was there?

"Here you go." The waitress appeared with a pan, sliding it to the center of the table. "Can I get you anything else?"

"Another round of waters, please," Jeff ordered, handing out plates already on the table.

Three plates.

There were three plates. I hadn't noticed before but . . .

Our gazes met. He'd asked for three plates in case I came tonight. My heart swelled, so full it threatened to burst.

When was the last time someone had *hoped* for me?

"Can I have two pieces?" Katy's question broke the moment, snaring Jeff's attention.

He took two slices of pizza from the pan, lifted them to her plate and used his fork to pick off the olives.

This man doted on his daughter. He didn't spoil her, just loved.

"Thank you," I said as Jeff handed me my plate loaded with two slices.

We ate in an easy silence, the noise from the restaurant a backdrop to the meal. Katy continued to color on her page as she chewed, then challenged me to a game of tic-tac-toe. And though I was full, I hated the sight of my empty plate. I wasn't ready to go home yet to a lonely house.

"Should we head home?" Jeff asked her after paying the check—refusing when I'd offered to chip in.

"Do you want to come over for game night?" Katy clasped my forearm. "Pleasepleasepleasepleaseplease. It would be way more fun with three people. When it's just me and

Daddy we can only pick from like, four games and if I have to play cribbage again I might die. It's his favorite but it's boring."

Jeff huffed. "Gee. Thanks."

She ignored him. "Have you ever played Ticket to Ride? It's this train game and it's so much fun. Or we could play Settlers of Catan. It's my other favorite."

"Katy, I'm sure Miss Ad—"

"I'm in."

Reckless. Foolish. But I really wanted to go to game night. "Is that okay?" I asked Jeff.

"Yeah." He looked like he was fighting a smile. "More than okay. Let's go."

"One thing." I held up a finger. "Katy, it's probably best that the other kids in your class don't know I'm coming to game night."

"Oh, because they'd get jealous."

"Exactly." And because I'd lose my job.

She pretended to zip her lips shut, then let out a giggle. "Ticket to Ride first. Then Settlers."

"I'll just follow you." I slid out of the booth behind her, snagging my coat. Then I followed them outside, climbing in my Jeep as they loaded into Jeff's truck.

What was I doing? This was far beyond a *coincidental* meeting. But I stayed close to his truck, not wanting to miss a single turn as he led the way home.

His house wasn't far from my place, ten blocks at most. I parked behind him on the street, taking in the charming, cottage-style house with gray siding and white trim. The front door was wooden with a large, marbled-glass inset. The second floor had a peaked roof, a square window in the triangle's face, and beside it a cute dormer.

The landscaping was simple with a row of hedges beneath

the porch railing. But otherwise, it was just a yard, similar to his neighbors'.

Katy beat both Jeff and me to the porch, waving us to hurry inside.

"Want something to drink?" he asked, hanging up my coat.

"Water."

"Make yourself at home." He left me in the entryway, his boots thudding on the hardwood floors as he disappeared around a corner.

"We play in here." Katy took my hand, dragging me through the first open doorway to my left into a dining room.

In its center was a table and six chairs situated below a glass and brass chandelier. Katy went to the buffet against the far wall, opening a cupboard that was stuffed with games.

As she rifled around, I spun in a slow circle, taking in their house. It was older with a classic layout, designed and built before open concept had become so popular. I loved that each room had four walls.

The floors were new—the home had been remodeled and updated—but there were still pieces that seemed original, like the intricate trim around the doorways.

Tacked to the wall adjacent the buffet was a framed chalkboard. Jeff and Katy had written out a list of their games on one side. Then they'd broken it into two columns, one for *Dad* and another for *Dandelion*. A scoreboard.

Jeff strode into the room with three glasses of water, setting them on the table.

"She's kicking your butt," I said, nodding to the scoreboard.

He winked. "Yeah, she's cutthroat."

"What does that mean?" Katy asked.

"Means you never let me win."

"Why would I let you win, Daddy?"

He reached out and tugged a lock of her hair. "Don't let me win."

"I won't." Yeah, this girl was cutthroat. I loved it. I laughed. I could spend hours listening to these two banter.

So I did.

We played games until darkness had long fallen outside. Until Katy yawned too many times to hide.

"Okay, time for a shower and bed," he told her.

"But—"

He cut her off with a pointed finger to the ceiling. "Say good night to Miss Adler."

"You're leaving already?"

"Yeah." I nodded, even though leaving was the last thing I wanted to do. "I'd better get home."

"Well, thanks for coming over." Katy rounded the table, stopping beside my chair for a hug. "That was really fun."

"Yes, it was. Thanks for inviting me."

She smiled at her dad, then skipped to the staircase.

As we put away the games, the water turned on above us. "Thank you," I told Jeff. "I haven't had a fun Friday night in . . . a long time."

"Better than cleaning?"

"Marginally."

He chuckled, that deep, rich laugh I'd heard all night. It was addicting and unsatisfying all at the same time. Every time he laughed, I needed more. But he sobered too quickly, putting the lid on the game. "What's the situation with the school? How big of a deal is this?"

"There are no rules against a friendship."

"And what if I wanted more than friendship?" He relaxed in his chair, holding my gaze for a long moment. There was desire in his eyes. In his voice. Never in my life had anyone so clearly *wanted* me. Certainly not Luka.

Yes, I wanted more than friendship. I wanted it so badly I ached. But . . .

"It's not allowed. Not while Katy is my student."

"All right." He leaned forward, elbows to knees. "Friends."

"Friends." I forced a smile despite my sinking heart. Standing, I made my way to the entryway, every step heavy like my shoes were wading through wet concrete.

Jeff followed, taking my coat off the hook where he'd hung it earlier. Then he held it open, but instead of sliding my arms inside, I inched closer.

"What if I wanted more than friendship?" I whispered.

What if I wanted him to kiss me? Right here. Right now.

No one in the world would have to know. Just . . . us.

His eyes flared, his arms dropping to his sides, my coat still clutched in a hand. "Della," he warned. "You're shredding my willpower here. You'd better go before it snaps."

"Then give me my coat."

He didn't move.

So I closed the gap between us, feeling bold for the first time in my life. He made me comfortable enough to do that. To break the rules. To throw caution to the wind and just be desired.

His scent, citrus with woodsy undertones, invaded my nose. Damn, but he smelled good.

I was seconds away from rising up on my toes and pressing a kiss to the corner of his mouth when footsteps pounded down the stairs.

Jeff ran a hand over his face, stepping back.

I did the same, putting a foot between us as Katy

appeared at the base of the staircase wearing *Star Wars* pajamas, her hair wet and combed.

"Bye, Miss Adler."

"Bye, Katy." My throat was dry, my voice scratchy. I reached for my coat, trying to take it from Jeff's hand, but his fist clamped on the fabric, holding it for a long second before finally giving it up.

I put it on, hating its weight as it settled on my shoulders. Then with a wave, I turned and opened the door, stepping into the night.

Wishing I didn't have to go home.

seven
Della

I was halfway down the sidewalk when Jeff's door opened behind me. My heart climbed into my throat as I turned.

"Della." Jeff's frame was limned in light from inside. His hands were shoved in his jean pockets, accentuating the silhouette of his broad shoulders. He seemed so impossibly large, like a tree I wanted to climb.

Go home, Della.

My feet didn't budge.

"Can you just . . ." He tugged a hand from his pocket to rake through his hair. "Good night."

My heart went *splat* on the sidewalk. "Good night."

With a turn, it took every effort not to let my shoulders slump as I trudged to the Jeep. Why had I expected anything else? I'd just told him I could get in trouble at work if we had a relationship. He'd backed off, said we could be friends.

And friends went home after game night. They didn't linger in entryways for a kiss.

God, how long had it been since I'd kissed a man?

Too long. I'd been foolishly waiting on Luka to open his eyes.

"Freaking Luka," I muttered, digging my keys from my pocket.

"What?"

I whirled around.

Jeff stood three feet away.

My palm pressed against my racing heart. "What are you doing?"

Jeff glanced over his shoulder to the still open front door. No sign of Katy other than the glowing light from the upstairs dormer window. "Can you wait?"

Yep. I was good at waiting. To my own goddamn detriment. But this summer wasn't far away. Just a couple months and we could explore this.

"You could go around back. Hang in the yard for a few until I get Katy to bed."

"Oh. You mean wait tonight?"

"Tonight. Just . . . I want longer with you."

Was I really doing this? "All right."

Even in the darkness, the smile that stretched across his mouth made my pulse spike. It would be so disappointing if I didn't have those lips on mine, at least once.

Jeff hooked a thumb over his shoulder. "Follow the path past the garage."

"Okay."

He smiled wider, then turned and jogged to the porch, taking the stairs two at a time before vanishing inside and closing the door.

I lingered on the sidewalk for a few long moments, taking in the front of his house. My hands dove into my coat pockets as I shrugged it further up my neck, not from the cold, but from nerves.

Not a soul would need to know about tonight. No matter what happened, this could be our secret.

Especially if Katy thought I was on my way home.

The light upstairs dimmed to just a faint glow, like there was a nightlight in her room. I counted to fifty, then followed the sidewalk toward the detached garage, taking the path along its side to the yard in the back.

I'd expected darkness, maybe a patio or something. But a golden glimmer welcomed me to a space bordered by a tall wooden fence. And above my head, fairy lights.

I tipped my head back, taking in the strings. Beyond the bulbs, stars peeked down from the midnight sky.

"Wow." The lights formed a perfect pattern, like the lines on a seashell, fanning from a single point—the corner of the garage. From that spot, they ran to the eaves of Jeff's house.

Along the back edge of the yard, tucked against the fence, was a massive cottonwood tree. From its lowest branches hung lanterns.

A partially constructed firepit sat in the opposite corner from the house, the bricks scattered and loose. A pallet of pavers was close by, resting beside bags of sand.

It wasn't a large space but with the fence and tree, it was intimate. Sheltered. The promise of a sanctuary.

I was on my second turn through the space, imagining what Jeff would do, when he stepped out of the patio door, striding across the small concrete pad to join me in the grass.

"This is beautiful." I waved to the lights.

"Not yet. But someday." He crossed his arms over his chest, glancing up at the tree's branches, still bare from winter, but soon they'd bud with spring leaves. "It was this tree that sold me on the house. I had this idea that it would be the backdrop for Katy's big moments. Sweet sixteen. Her graduation party. Maybe even a rehearsal dinner someday."

Oh, he was the best dad. He had no idea how attractive it was, did he? "What will you do back here?"

"I want twice as many lights. Not so many that it's bright, but enough that you can take photos without a flash." He walked to the tree, placing his palm on its rough bark. "I have another box of lanterns for this, enough to go up about thirty feet."

"Wow."

He smacked the tree, then pointed to the firepit, walking in the same slow circle I'd taken around the space. "That will be a sitting area with a ledge. Then a border of pavers all around. I might even get rid of the grass altogether and just put in planters. We'll see. I've got a thousand ideas."

"Like what?" I clung to his every word as he spoke. I followed him like he was a planet and I was a moon, dragged along in his orbit.

"This is probably boring as hell," he said after our third lap. "Sorry."

"It's not."

Jeff stopped just beyond the patio, turning to face me.

I stopped too, standing just within arm's reach.

He reached up, tucking a lock of hair behind my ear. "I'm stalling."

"You're stalling."

"You gotta tell me what you want. It's your job. It's your life. You want to wait until summer, then I'll walk you to your car right now."

I inched closer. More of that bravery bubbled to the surface. Was this a stupid idea? Yep. So why couldn't I leave? "What if I don't want to go to my car?"

A growl came from his chest as he dragged a hand over his jaw. "You're sure?"

"Is Katy asleep?"

He nodded once. "Out like a light."

"Then I want you to kiss me."

The words were barely out of my mouth before his lips crushed mine, his strong arms sweeping me off my feet as he hauled me into his chest.

Yes. Whatever doubts I had vanished. I melted against him, sinking into the feel of those lips against mine. Never in my life had I been this bold. Never in my life had I told a man to kiss me.

Worth it. So fucking worth it.

His tongue swept against the seam of my lips, demanding entry. A mewl escaped my throat as he slid inside. Then he plundered, fluttering and tangling and swirling his tongue with mine until I was breathless.

This man could *kiss*. Thank the stars in the sky, he could kiss.

He nipped at the corner of my mouth, then sucked my bottom lip between his teeth. He slanted over me, delving deeper, leaving no corner of my mouth untouched.

My entire body went up in flames, my pulse thudding in time with the aching throb in my core. When he broke us apart, my lips were swollen. He latched on to my neck, sucking and kissing as he left a trail down the column of my throat.

"More." I fisted the material of his shirt, holding him to me.

"Fuck, Della." His voice held an edge of restraint, like he was trying to press the brakes. He pulled back, setting me on my feet. His eyes searched mine and his Adam's apple bobbed as he swallowed hard. Then he shifted, taking a step away.

No. "Don't," I panted.

Maybe it was the years of rejection from Luka. Maybe it was this all-consuming need for Jeff's touch, his skin against mine. If I had to beg, I'd beg. Tonight, I wanted to be craved.

Worshiped. And if that kiss was any indication, together, we could be dynamite.

"Della—"

"Please don't pull away from me." There was a vulnerability in my voice that surprised even me.

Jeff's eyes softened. "I don't want to, beautiful. But if I don't put this space between us, I'm not sure I'll be able to let you go."

The air rushed from my lungs. *He wants me.* Deep down, I knew he wanted me. That kiss was a kiss from a man who wanted a woman. But to hear the need in his voice, well . . . it meant I didn't care about the rules. Not tonight.

I'd risk it all, just once.

"You said I had to tell you what I want," I said. "And that's you. Kiss me again. Take me inside to your bedroom. Or if all you want to do is sit at the table and play cribbage with me, I'll take whatever I can get. We don't even know each other but the idea of me leaving right now . . ." I shook my head. "I don't want to leave."

"If we go inside, it sure as fuck won't be to play cribbage."

My heart skipped. "Then take me inside."

We stared at each other, the lights above us bright enough that I could read the hesitation in his gaze. Then his expression shifted, and the restraint was gone. He surged. One long stride and I was in his arms again, his mouth crushing mine.

I hummed, sinking into this kiss, closing my eyes to savor his taste. My toes skimmed the ground as he walked us toward the house.

One of his arms shifted beneath my ass, hoisting me up, and my legs wrapped around his hips, my center pressed against the hardness beneath his jeans.

He growled against my mouth, tearing his lips away as he reached for the door. When we stepped inside, he flipped off the lights, inside and out, bathing us in darkness. Then with both hands, he palmed my ass and rocked my core against his arousal.

"Yes," I hissed.

"Kiss me, Della," he murmured, an edge to that gravelly voice.

I leaned in, latching on to his throat, dragging my tongue against his skin. It earned me another groan as he carried us down a hallway before closing us in his bedroom.

His spicy scent filled the air, like earth and orange peel and cedar. When I left here, I wanted that smell in my hair so I could breathe it in for hours.

"You smell so good," I whispered against his jaw.

He buried his nose in my hair, inhaling my perfume. Then we were falling, my back landing on a soft mattress as his weight settled on top of mine.

"More." I pulled at the flannel of his shirt, wanting it gone.

He lifted up, stripping it off along with the shirt beneath while I kicked off my shoes. "Another night, I'll strip you out of those clothes slow. I'll tease you for hours, baby."

My pussy clenched. Yes, please. "But not tonight."

Tonight, I wanted fast and hard. I wanted to feel alive.

"No." He flicked the button on my jeans, then ripped them from my legs with a fast swoosh. "Not tonight."

I scrambled to sit up, tugging the hem of my own shirt to fling it from my body.

Then Jeff's hand swatted mine away so he could flick the clasp on my bra. His hands cupped my naked breasts, his thumbs rubbing my pebbled nipples.

"More." I arched into his touch.

He replaced his hands with his hot mouth, closing his lips around a nipple and sucking. Hard.

"More." My hands dove into his hair as he toyed with me, threading my fingers through the soft strands.

He left a wet trail across my heart as he gave the other nipple the same attention. Then he released it with a pop to plant a hand on my sternum and push me onto my back.

"Fuck, you're perfect." He took my panties off with a single pull, the flimsy lace sailing over his shoulder. Then his mouth was on me, fucking me with his tongue.

"Oh my God." I arched off the bed, the sheer pleasure of his head between my legs blanking my mind.

"You taste so fucking sweet, Della." He lapped at my center before sucking my clit.

"Yes." I fisted the bedding beside me, the world already fading to a blur. There was nothing but his tongue and the breathy moans escaping my throat as tingles spread across my skin.

Heat pooled, lapping higher and higher and higher, until I shattered, coming on a cry as he feasted, drawing out the longest, hardest orgasm of my life. Every muscle in my body quaked while my head rocketed to the stars. Then I floated down to reality, sending a silent *thank you* to the heavens for this dream of a man.

Jeff kissed the inside of my thigh so tenderly it made my breath hitch.

"More," I whimpered.

Not even that orgasm was enough to satisfy this need for him. This ache to be filled and fucked.

The last time I'd had sex was a year ago. And God, it hadn't been like this. Not even close. At the time, I'd thought it would never be better.

What a fool. I hadn't even known what I was missing.

The sound of a zipper filled the room followed by the plop of Jeff's jeans hitting the floor. When I cracked my eyes open, he was standing at the foot of the bed in all his naked glory, his hand fisted around his cock.

"Um . . ." My eyes bugged out. "You're . . ."

Huge. I'd been so focused on his perfect ass that I hadn't even stopped to think about what he was packing in the front.

My mouth watered and I pushed up on an elbow, wanting to feel him in my hand. Wanting to taste him on my tongue.

"Another night." But he shook his head, planting a knee in the bed before reaching to the nightstand and retrieving a condom. When it was on, he settled into the cradle of my hips, that enormous cock heavy against my sensitive flesh.

"Promise there will be another night?" I needed to know this wasn't a one-time thing. That he wanted me enough to do this again and again.

"Promise." He nuzzled his jaw into my neck, the scrape of his stubble delicious against my skin. He dragged his arousal through my center, teasing. Then he positioned himself at my entrance, and with a smooth stroke, he slid inside.

My eyes drifted closed, the build of another orgasm beginning again as I stretched around him. "You feel . . ."

"So fucking good." He angled his hips, driving impossibly deep.

My eyes flew open to see the sheer pleasure on his face.

He eased out and thrust inside again, hard and fast. My inner walls began to flutter, that orgasm barreling toward me without control.

Jeff took my legs, pressing my knees wide. Then he pistoned his hips, setting a rhythm that had me writhing beneath him. The thickness of his cock. The rough scrape of his calloused hands on my skin. The combination was enough to drive me wild.

"Come, Della." He drove inside me, until the root of his shaft pressed against my clit.

I cried out, my back coming off the bed as I exploded once more. Stars broke behind my eyes, and I got lost. Lost in this man as he fucked me relentlessly.

He worked us together, stroke by stroke, until he tipped his head to the ceiling, letting out a groan as his body shook and tensed with his own release. Then he collapsed on top of me, our skin sticky with sweat as our hearts thundered in opposite rhythms.

"Wow," I whispered, shoving a damp lock of hair off my forehead.

He hummed, rolling us together so I wasn't crushed beneath his weight. Then he positioned me on his chest, holding me close. "Fuck, Della. That was . . ."

Dynamite. "Yeah."

"Give me five." His large hand drifted down my spine. "Then we're doing that again."

I giggled. "Okay."

My hands drifted down his back, my palms pressing into his skin until they came to his ass. As imagined, it was firm, round and perfect. So I did something I'd wanted to do for weeks.

I gave it a good squeeze.

eight
Jeff

"Drive careful," I murmured against Della's hair as we stood next to the open front door.

"It's ten blocks," she said, keeping her voice low. Her breath fanned across my bare chest. Her hands were on my hips, her fingertips light against my skin.

We'd woken up about twenty minutes ago and while she'd dressed in yesterday's clothes, all I'd bothered with were my jeans. They were unbuttoned, hanging loose on my hips.

The morning air was cold as it seeped inside, but last night, I'd learned that Della had a thing for my abs. Not as much as she liked my ass, but enough that I wanted her to get a good look before she left today.

A tease, because damn it, I needed her to come back.

"Text me later?" I asked.

"Yeah." She eased away, rising up on her toes for a kiss.

I framed her face in my hands and took that pretty mouth, kissing her until her face was flushed. As much as she liked my body, I fucking loved how easily she blushed. Everywhere.

"I'd better go." She peered past me, checking to make sure we were alone.

It was five in the morning and I had no doubt that Katy was fast asleep. She rarely woke before six thirty, and on a Saturday, that kid's internal clock had a three-hour snooze. But just in case, Della was taking off before we risked a run-in with my daughter.

It was one thing to ask Katy to keep a pizza and game night to herself. It was another not to slip that she'd seen her teacher sneak out of her dad's bedroom one morning.

"Bye." With a kiss on her forehead, I stood in the threshold, watching as she hurried down the sidewalk to her Jeep. Then she gave me a finger wave before pulling away from the curb and disappearing down the block.

I sighed, dragging a hand through my hair as I closed the door. Then I let free the smile I'd been holding captive. That certainly hadn't been what I'd expected last night. But even if I'd hoped for it, nothing could have prepared me for Della. The way my body came alive, the way hers responded, was like nothing I'd felt before.

We'd stayed up most of the night exploring each other's bodies. Della was ticklish behind her knees. She made the sexiest fucking sound when I nipped at her earlobe. She was gorgeous, but when she came, that woman was breathtaking.

A smile tugged at my mouth as I made my way to the bedroom, her sweet, floral perfume still clinging to the air. I found a sweatshirt and tugged it on, then buttoned my jeans before padding to the kitchen for coffee. A shower was calling but I wasn't quite ready to wash Della off my skin.

Maybe once I was sure I could get that scent back.

We hadn't talked about when we'd see each other again, but it would be soon. It had to be soon. Now that I'd had her, I needed more.

As my coffee brewed, I stood at the patio door, taking in the yard under the gray hues of twilight. I hadn't shown the yard to anyone before, just Katy. Maybe because I didn't have a lot of friends.

My colleagues at work were the closest thing to friends I had, but they were still colleagues. Hans and I were close but he was still my boss. None of us shared much outside of work, mostly because my world revolved around Katy. Making friends had never been a priority.

Or maybe the reason I hadn't shown anyone this project was because it was nothing to be proud of. Not yet.

But it could be. Having Della here last night made me want to transform this space. Turn it into the place I'd told her about. A sanctuary. I wanted to see it through her dazzling caramel eyes when it was finished.

So I filled a coffee mug, sipping it carefully until it cooled, then found a pair of boots and trudged outside, making a plan for the weekend.

By the time Katy came downstairs dressed in her pajamas, her hair a disheveled nest, I'd made a list for a trip to the greenhouse and had a plan for the firepit.

"Hi, Daddy." She yawned, shuffling through the dining room toward my chair. Like she did most weekends here, she crawled in my lap and rested her cheek on my shoulder.

She still fit here, my girl. When she was little, she'd snuggle with me for as long as I'd hold her. I hadn't appreciated it then, too rushed to get her breakfast or move along with the day. Now she was twelve, and I could see the end of this road: the days when she'd no longer want to cuddle with her dad on a Saturday morning.

So I held her tighter until she shifted and stood, glancing around the dining room. "It was fun having Miss Adler here last night."

"It sure was." More than I'd planned for. What a damn night.

"Do you think she'll come back?" Katy asked.

"Hope so." I hoped like hell.

There was a chance that reality would sink in today. That she'd realize how much she was risking. That she'd decide I wasn't worth it.

Had I pushed too hard? *Maybe.* But when she'd given me permission, when she'd asked for a kiss, I hadn't been able to stop. If we could just keep this a secret for a couple more months until the end of the school year, it wouldn't matter, right?

Just a couple months, then we'd be free to really explore this thing.

There weren't many times in my life when I'd felt the world rock beneath my feet. The first had been Katy. She'd come into my life on a wail and had changed me completely. Della had snuck up on me, but there was no doubt the world had shifted again last night.

She'd felt it too, right? The temptation to find out was nearly crippling. My phone was heavy in my pocket, but I refused to dig for it. Not yet. I'd text Della later, but not yet.

So I stood from my chair and made my daughter breakfast. After we'd eaten and the dishes were done, I told her to run upstairs and get dressed while I put on a clean pair of jeans. Then we drove to my favorite local nursery to get some supplies.

"Daddy, can I buy this for my room?" Katy held up a small potted succulent from a stand on the path to the checkout line.

"Sure," I said as my phone rang.

My heart jumped as I hoped for Della's name. But it was Rosalie. I bit back a curse and answered. "Hello."

"Can I talk to her?"

Why Rosalie refused to call Katy's number on the week-ends when she was with me I'd never understand. But I held out the phone, keeping a snide comment to myself. "It's your mom."

"Hey, Mom," Katy answered. "He told me that you were *sick*."

There was as much skepticism in her voice as I felt in my soul, so I turned away, not wanting Katy to catch me smirking.

"That's okay, Mom. I'm good to just hang with Dad today."

Then Rosalie must have asked her something she didn't like because her nose scrunched up. But then she nodded. "Okay. I'll see you then. Bye." Katy held out the phone.

"What did she say?" I asked.

"That she was still sick today, but tomorrow, she wants me to come over since I didn't get my full time with her."

Damn. "Let's just see how she feels."

"Yeah." Katy sighed.

Eventually, maybe she'd start to refuse Rosalie. But she wasn't at the point yet where she'd tell her mother no.

If Katy didn't want to spend time over there, then it was Rosalie's problem to figure out why. Maybe one day, Rosalie would realize that Katy wasn't the type of kid content to spend her weekends watching TV for hours and hours on end. She was happiest if there was an activity, like a game or even a trip to the nursery.

"Are you going to help me when we get home?" I asked, pushing the cart toward the cashier.

"What are we doing?"

"Building a firepit."

"Yes. Can we roast marshmallows?"

"Probably won't get that far today but maybe by tomorrow."

"Are you going to pay me?"

"Yeah." I pointed to her plant. "That's your payment."

"Daddy." She scoffed. "Seriously?"

"Did you want that plant or . . ."

She debated it during the entire checkout process until the cashier gave her a pointed look and she placed it on the counter, a new addition to the twenty other mini plants in her bedroom.

Katy usually remembered to water them, but during the weeks she was at her mother's, I made sure to keep her little bedroom garden alive and flourishing.

When we got home, she helped me unload supplies, but her help on the firepit lasted only an hour before she went inside for a water break and never returned.

Meanwhile after every two bricks I stacked, I checked my phone, hoping for something from Della. And got nothing.

Worry started to build, twisting and knotting in my gut. Did she regret last night? Fuck, I hoped not.

After another thirty minutes and still no text from Della, I took a water break of my own, then I went upstairs to find Katy.

She was in her room, lounging in the chair swing that I'd given her on her birthday.

"Hey." I leaned against the door, rapping my knuckles on the jamb.

Katy gasped, slamming closed the diary she'd been writing in and moving so fast she nearly toppled to the floor.

"Easy." I took a step forward, too late to catch her, but she caught herself before she crashed.

"You scared me." She tucked the diary beneath the chair's pillow cushion.

What had she been writing about? She probably had a crush. *Hell.* I wasn't ready for crushes. Not yet.

We'd have to have "the talk" sooner or later. I wasn't leaving that one to Rosalie. But not at twelve. Not yet.

"What are you doing?" I asked her.

"Just writing in my diary."

I regretted giving her that diary now. Especially if it contained hearts and doodles.

My head began to spin.

No crushes. Period. The only person in this house allowed to have a crush was me.

"Are you going to come back outside and help?"

Katy shook her head. "Nah."

"So you're just going to be up here."

"Yep."

"Oh." I turned and walked out the door, stopping just outside the threshold.

When I looked back, Katy was watching. Waiting. "Can you close the door?"

I frowned. But did I close the door? Yes. I wanted her to have her privacy. Still, I stomped down the stairs, too loud, casting a glance to the ceiling every few steps.

She was hiding something. Katy never hid anything from me. But she was definitely hiding something. What was in that diary?

"Ugh." I scrubbed a hand over my face and retreated outside, staring at the half-completed firepit. These were the times when I wished Rosalie and I were on better terms. That I could get a woman's perspective. "Fuck it."

I pulled my phone from my pocket and dialed Della's number, pressing it to my ear. Maybe she'd know if something was happening with Katy at school. Though mostly, I just wanted to hear her voice.

It rang three times before she answered, sounding out of breath. "Hello."

"Hey."

"Hi." That whisper was followed by five agonizing heartbeats of silence.

Della hadn't called me today. She hadn't texted.

Yep, she was regretting last night. *Shit.*

"Listen, about last night—"

"Della!" A man's voice echoed in the background. "Let's go, baby."

Baby.

What the fuck?

nine
Della

"Jeff?" No reply. I pulled the phone from my ear. "Damn it."

He'd hung up.

I growled, frustration rippling through my every cell.

As much as I wanted to call him back, it would have to wait. First, I needed to deal with my infuriating roommate. So I stormed out of my bedroom, stopping at the top of the staircase to glare down at Luka.

He was standing at the bottom of the steps. No way that was where he'd yelled from a moment ago. He'd been up here, probably lurking outside my door.

I fisted my hands on my hips. "Baby?"

"What?"

"You called me baby."

"So?"

My nostrils flared. "Don't call me baby."

Effective last night, the only man who was calling me *baby* was Jeff.

"Can we go?" Luka asked, tapping his foot. "I'm starving and want to pick up a sandwich or something at the store."

"Go by yourself." I spun on a heel and marched to my room, slamming the door so hard it rattled the photo of me and my parents hanging on the wall. Then I threw my phone on the bed and rubbed at my temples.

The day had started off so well. Morning sex with Jeff, then a kiss at the door. I'd driven home giddy, riding the high of last night. Then I'd walked inside my home only to be accosted by Luka.

He'd been on the couch wearing a pair of sweats, a cup of coffee in one hand and his phone in the other. He'd had the nerve to look hurt, glowering while he drank out of *my* favorite mug.

I'd ignored him, coming upstairs to take a power nap. Then after a couple hours, I'd gotten up to shower and get dressed. When I'd gone down to the kitchen to make a late breakfast and have some coffee myself, Luka had been in the exact same spot, still glowering.

Finally, after I'd eaten and was rinsing my dishes, he'd come shuffling into the kitchen. The glower was gone, replaced with a pathetic pout.

When he'd asked me where I'd spent the night, I'd told him it was none of his damn business.

Since I'd skipped cleaning to be with Jeff last night, I'd decided to at least hit the kitchen and my bathroom. Instead of disappearing to his room like he normally did when I took out the Windex and Soft Scrub, Luka had hovered, insisting on helping dust, vacuum and mop the floors.

His pouting didn't stop, and with it, he started prodding for information on where I'd spent last night.

You're seeing Rogers, aren't you?

Rogers was the middle school gym teacher. He was cute, though the shaved-head look wasn't for me. Plus, Rogers was ten years older than me and divorced. Occasionally, the two of us would sit together in the teachers' lounge for lunch and Luka loved to tease because Rogers did have a crush on me.

I'd refused to say a word, so I'd just kept on cleaning.

He'd kept on talking.

By the time the main floor was clean and my bathroom gleamed, I'd been ready to shove the toilet bowl brush down Luka's mouth, anything to shut him up.

Then I'd made the mistake of saying I was going to the grocery store. He'd volunteered to come along and I hadn't had the energy to tell him no. I'd just come upstairs for socks and shoes when my phone had rung.

Luka must have overheard, and he'd pulled that *baby* stunt.

"Asshole."

He was jealous. No question. Luka was jealous. And that was as infuriating as anything else.

How many women had he paraded in front of me? How many times had he made it clear that I was only his friend? Just a roommate who helped share living costs?

He didn't get to be jealous. He didn't get to screw this up with Jeff.

I pulled up my recent calls and hit Jeff's number but it went straight to voicemail. "Shit."

We had enough working against us. We were new. We'd be a secret. I didn't need Luka creating unnecessary bullshit simply because I wasn't going to pine after him.

Not anymore.

I'd wasted too many years on him already.

The realization was freeing. I shook my head, barking a dry laugh.

He wasn't good enough for me. Oddly enough, my dad

had said that once. He'd told me that any man who didn't see the beauty that was living under his roof was an idiot.

Had I listened? No. So who was the actual idiot at this address?

Me.

I tried Jeff again, but when it went to his voicemail for the second time, I put on my socks and shoes, then jogged downstairs.

Luka was back on the couch again. So much for his trip to the store. "Della."

"What?"

"Where are you going?"

"None of your damn business." Maybe if I said it enough, he'd back off.

"Come on. Don't be like that. Let's go to the store. Then maybe we can go do something fun."

"No, thanks." I snagged my coat from its hook, shrugging it on.

"It's that parent, isn't it? That dad you kept checking out. That's who you were with last night."

I froze, my heart leaping into my throat. *Shit. Fuck.*

If Luka suspected, how hard would it be for anyone else to figure it out? I unstuck my feet, opening the door to rush outside—leaving with another slammed door. My legs felt unsteady but I pushed forward, walking to the Jeep and climbing inside.

It was just a guess, right? Luka couldn't know about Jeff. And as long as I kept quiet, we'd be fine. That was, if Jeff even wanted to see me again.

Fucking Luka.

The drive to Jeff's took only minutes, not long enough for my heart to stop racing. But I parked in the same place I'd been last night, and with my shoulders squared, I crossed the sidewalk to the porch steps.

If Katy asked why I was here, I'd say I lost my phone. Or keys. Or hair tie. With a fortifying breath, I reached for the bell, but before I could press the button, the door opened and Jeff filled its frame.

Yep, he was mad.

That chiseled jaw flexed as he crossed his arms across his chest.

"Hi."

He arched an eyebrow.

I tried to glance past him but he filled the threshold almost entirely. No surprise. I'd spent last night sleeping on that body and soaking in every broad inch. "Is Katy here?"

"No. One of the neighborhood kids just stopped by and asked if she could play." He jerked his chin down the block. "They're riding bikes."

"Okay." *Phew.* "Can I come in?"

Another eyebrow arch.

"That was Luka. Earlier, when we were on the phone."

"Figured as much."

"There's nothing going on between us. He did that because he's jealous."

"I don't want drama, Della."

"I teach middle school. I don't need more drama."

Jeff stood statue still, not so much as a blink. Did he think I was using him? Maybe to make Luka jealous? Or maybe that I was seeing them both?

I gulped. Then because I had a lot to lose by downplaying the truth—*Jeff*—I let the whole story come pouring out. Today, it was my turn to overshare.

"I liked him. For a long time. It started in college as a crush and it just never went away. I realize it's pathetic. I spent a long time waiting for him to see me. Once, I thought that if we lived together, he'd realize I was right there. That I'd been standing right there for years."

Jeff's arms uncrossed but he didn't say a word.

A good thing. If he stopped me, I probably wouldn't start again.

But I'd never told another soul on earth this next part, so I closed my eyes. Because if I had to see him pity me, I might not recover.

"About a year ago, I was having a rough day. One of my students was bullying another classmate and it escalated to the point where parents got involved. They accused me of overlooking the issue and not reacting soon enough. Maybe they were right. Regardless, one of the boys transferred out of our school and the other was removed from my classroom. I came home that night and decided a bottle of wine was in order."

My principal hadn't blamed me for the incident. She'd assured me that I'd done everything correctly, but it had still hurt. Seeing that boy break down because he'd been ridiculed and teased and I hadn't stopped it in time had broken my heart.

"Luka was there for me. He let me cry on his shoulder and held me when I needed to be held. He tried to cheer me up. It worked. And we . . ." I cringed. "We had sex."

Bland, mediocre sex.

At the time, I'd thought it was good. But as of last night, Jeff had taught me that not all orgasms were created equal. With Luka, there'd been no stars. No explosions. No curled toes or full-body tremors. With Luka, it had been mechanical, like the orgasms delivered by the vibrator in my nightstand.

"I've never told anyone that before," I whispered, my eyes still closed. "The next day, it was awkward. He said he didn't want to risk our friendship. That maybe we shouldn't have crossed that line because our relationship was too special to risk over a drunken, raw night. I was relieved and hurt all at the same time."

I'd waited years for him to see me and he'd finally, *finally* picked me. Then he'd shoved me back across the friend-zone boundary. From that point forward, my crush had begun to wither. I hadn't realized just how dead it had become until last night.

My feelings for Luka weren't feelings at all. It had just been easier to keep pretending. Because if I had an imaginary crush on him, then I didn't have to put myself out there for others. I could spend my Friday nights cleaning.

Or maybe I'd just been waiting on a man to snap me out of this coma.

"Della." Jeff's voice was smooth. Gentle. "Open your eyes."

I cracked one open.

Okay, he wasn't looking at me like I was a complete fool. That was something, right?

"Both eyes, baby."

I sighed and opened both eyes, then shrugged. "I like it when you call me baby. Luka has never called me baby in his life. And I told him never to do it again."

Jeff's eyes gentled as his hand came out to cup my cheek. "Do you want him?"

"Not even a little bit."

Maybe after all this time, that should have come with a bit of heartache. But I'd said goodbye to Luka a long time ago, even if I hadn't realized it yet.

"You're sure?"

I leaned into Jeff's touch. "I want you."

His thumb stroked my cheek. Then his hand slid to my nape and with one hard tug, he hauled me inside, slamming his mouth on mine the moment we were across the threshold.

With a quick kick of his foot, the door slammed closed behind us, then his tongue tangled with mine, his fingers threading through my hair, tugging at the roots until I moaned.

There was nothing sweet or soft with this kiss. Not like last night's. When he nipped at my bottom lip, it had a bite. When his tongue moved, it was to devour. To claim.

So I claimed him right back. I fisted my hands in his shirt, tugging him closer, and met his ferocity with my own.

We kissed until the thud of shoes outside broke us apart.

I wiped my mouth dry as Jeff did the same, turning and making an adjustment to the growing bulge behind his jeans.

My cheeks flamed and a giggle threatened to escape, but I swallowed it down just as Katy burst through the front door wearing a bike helmet.

"Miss Adler!" She rushed to give me a quick hug, oblivious to my swollen lips. "What are you doing here?"

"Oh, I, uh, forgot my . . . my . . ." My what? What had I planned to say?

"My hair tie," I blurted at the same time Jeff said, "Her ChapStick."

"Huh?" Katy looked between the two of us. "What's ChapStick?"

That giggle I'd been holding back escaped.

Jeff rubbed a palm over his face, chuckling too. "It's Chap-Stick. For chapped lips."

"Lip balm," I said.

"Ohhh." Katy nodded. "Gotcha. Did you find it?"

I patted my coat pocket. "Well, I'd better get going."

"Unless you wanted to stay." Katy shrugged. "We could play a game."

"What about riding bikes with your friend?" I asked.

"Her legs got tired so she went home already."

Jeff walked to the open door, closing it since Katy hadn't. Then he gave me a wink his daughter couldn't see. "Stay."

I stayed.

All night long.

ten

Jeff

Della's hand trailed along my thigh beneath the sheet. Damn, but that was the best way to wake up. Hard and ready for the naked woman tucked into my side.

"I need to go." Her lips were a whisper against the shell of my ear.

Go? Absolutely not.

With a quick flip, I pinned her on her back, settling into her hips as I nuzzled her neck. "Not yet."

She hummed and looped her arms around my shoulders, arching into my mouth as I trailed my lips across her collarbone.

Stretching for the nightstand, I felt across the surface for a condom, except the table was empty. I lifted, squinting in the darkness of my bedroom. "Fuck."

"What?"

"I'm out of condoms." I pinched her side. "Your fault."

Another insatiable night and my limited stash was gone.

She giggled, her hands drifting down my spine before her palms squeezed my butt.

My woman liked my ass. To be fair, I liked hers too.

"What if we didn't use a condom?" She reached between us, fisting my shaft. "I'm on birth control. And you know how long it's been."

"It's been a while for me too."

She dragged the head of my cock through her wetness. "I want to feel you. Nothing between us."

Was she expecting an argument? With a thrust of my hips, I slid inside Della's tight, wet heat. "Fuck, you feel good, baby."

"Yes." She was already starting to flutter around my length. Her hands clamped on my hips, her nails digging in hard.

I pressed deeper, gritting my teeth. *Goddamn.* I wasn't going to last this morning. She felt too good.

"More." She tilted up her hips.

This woman. Always wanting more.

I'd give it to her. Every fucking day, I'd give her more.

I rocked into her again and again, drawing out those sexy mewls. Bringing that flush out on her cheeks and chest. I fucked her, lazy and slow, until she pulsed and came on a gasp, her entire body trembling as she detonated.

"Della." I groaned, burying my face in that silky hair as I followed her over the edge, pouring myself inside her body until I was spent.

She wrapped her arms and legs around me, trapping me so we stayed connected. "What are you doing to me?"

"What do you mean?"

"We've had more sex in the past two nights than I've had in my entire life."

I chuckled, my cock twitching inside her. "It's good, baby. It's really fucking good."

"How good?"

I leaned back, pushing the hair off her face. "Best I've ever had."

Those sparkling caramel eyes softened. "Really?"

"Really." I kissed the corner of her mouth. "You want more. I want more."

Not just sex. I just wanted—*needed*—more of Della.

We held each other, limbs entwined, until the alarm I'd set last night chimed, and I rolled over to shut it off.

With a sigh, Della slid out of bed and began picking up her clothes from the floor. Clothes I'd stripped off her last night inch by torturous inch, just like I'd promised.

I swung my legs over the edge of the bed, dragged a hand through my disheveled hair and, while Della was in the bathroom, pulled on a pair of sweats and a T-shirt.

Last night, after games, Panda Express delivery and more games, I'd sent Katy upstairs to shower. And like the night before, Della had slipped into the backyard, inspecting my progress on the firepit while I'd kissed Katy good night and waited for her to fall asleep.

Then Della and I had locked ourselves in my bedroom. She'd offered to leave around midnight, but by the time we'd gone at it again, it had been nearly two in the morning and I hadn't wanted her driving home at that hour. Not when the bars had just closed and there was the chance of drunk idiots on the road.

So I'd set my alarm for five, leaving us just a few hours of sleep together. It wasn't enough.

How was it that I'd just met this woman but I was already hooked? Maybe another guy, especially one with my history, would have put up his guard. Would have held up a hand and kept her at a distance.

But Della was . . . special.

Yesterday, hearing her rambled confession on the front

porch, I'd felt like an asshole for hanging up on her just because her pissant of a roommate called her baby. I should have listened.

There weren't a lot of people I trusted. I preferred a tight circle. But I'd make a space for Della.

She emerged from the bathroom, dressed with her hair tied in a messy knot.

I held out my hand, amazed at how perfectly hers fit into my palm. Then I led her to the door, kissing her in the entryway before watching as she climbed in that mint green Jeep and drove away.

Damn, but I was in trouble.

The best kind of trouble.

On a yawn, I headed for the kitchen and brewed some coffee. Then I headed outside to pick up where I'd left off on the firepit.

A few hours later, Katy came downstairs.

"Morning, Dandelion."

"Morning," she muttered with a frown.

"What's wrong?"

"I don't want to go to Mom's."

I didn't want her to go either. "It's just for the day."

"She had her chance but she got sick or whatever. I just want to hang out here today."

"I know."

Katy aimed those sad hazel eyes my way and I knew before she spoke what she'd say. "Do I have to?"

I nodded. "It's just for the day."

"Why?"

"Your mom won't get to see you for a week. Won't you miss her?"

"No. And it's not like you want me to go either, but you don't feel like fighting with Mom, so I have to go."

Ouch. Her truths were sharp this morning. "I'm sorry you don't want to go. It's not for long, then you'll be back. And you're right, I don't want to get in an argument with your mother."

"She ruins everything."

"Katy," I warned.

"It's true." She tossed out an arm. "Every time I'm having a good time she ruins it. Either she gets sick so we have to leave stuff early or I'm here and she wants me to come back. It's not fair."

No, it wasn't. But life wasn't fair.

"How about we go out to breakfast before heading over?" I hauled her into a hug and kissed her hair, then sent her upstairs to get dressed while I took a quick shower.

We went to our favorite café and an hour later, I dropped her at Rosalie's and went to Home Depot for more yard supplies. Anything to avoid going home to an empty house. It never got easier, leaving her, even if it was for a day.

But shopping only took a couple hours, and as expected, when I got home, it was too quiet. Too lonely. So I dug my phone from my pocket, hoping Della would help me fix that problem, but it rang with Katy's name on the screen.

"Hey, Dandelion."

She sniffled. "Can you come get me?"

"Katy, you've only been there for two hours."

"I'm not at Mom's."

The hairs on the back of my neck stood up. "Where are you?"

"The emergency room."

"Daddy!" Katy shot out of her chair in the ER's waiting room, running into my arms as I walked through the sliding doors.

"You okay?"

She nodded, her face buried in my stomach as her arms held tight. "I hate it here."

"I know you do." I kissed her hair, then unwound her from my waist, taking her hand as I walked toward the receptionist. "Rosalie Dawson?"

Rosalie had kept my last name, wanting to have the same name as Katy. I understood her reasoning, yet it felt like something she'd stolen, along with my money to pay for emergency room visits just like this.

The rage I'd built up on the drive over would undoubtedly last the rest of the week.

Why have Katy come to her house if she was going to pull this bullshit? She could have spared our daughter a visit to a place that reeked of antiseptic and illness.

While the receptionist made a call to the nurses past the ER's doors, I glanced around the room. A couple was huddled beside the windows. The woman was hacking and coughing so hard I feared she'd choke. Then there was a man slouched in a chair in the far corner, his clothes tattered and dirty, like he'd worn them for weeks, not days.

Not the place I wanted my kid to spend her Sunday.

"A nurse will be out in a minute," the receptionist said, motioning toward the doors that led into the ER. Doors I'd been through too many times.

Less than sixty seconds later—I counted, because Katy was not spending more than that minute here—a nurse walked out and called us forward. "Rosalie Dawson?"

I raised my free hand, then with Katy's grip firmly in mine, we followed the nurse into the ER, past a few empty exam stations and those where the curtains had been closed.

All the way to the end of the row, where she tugged back the partition, revealing Rosalie on a bed, eyes closed and resting on her side.

"Rosalie." I waited until she opened her eyes, then checked my anger.

She looked miserable. Maybe I should have gone in when I'd dropped off Katy earlier. Whether or not she was actually sick, it still wasn't fun to see her here, beneath a white hospital blanket, wearing a faded blue gown.

"What's wrong?" I asked.

"My stomach." She winced, like speaking the word made the pain worse. "It started hurting again."

"Have you seen a doctor?"

She nodded. "Just a minute ago. He's going to do an ultrasound to make sure it's not my appendix."

"All right. Can I get you anything?"

"No." She looked to Katy, her eyes welling with tears. "Sorry, honey."

"It's okay, Mom." Katy went over and gave her a hug. "I hope you feel better."

"Thanks."

I jerked my chin toward the hall. "Give me a minute, Dandelion."

Katy nodded, then shuffled outside the curtain, no doubt eavesdropping.

So I moved closer to Rosalie's bed, sitting on its side. "I'll take her home. Let me know what the doctor says."

She nodded, closing her eyes. A tear escaped. That was the hardest part of all this. Maybe she was sick. Maybe it was her appendix. Maybe she was fine.

I didn't know what to do for her. I never had. In moments like this, part of me wished we were on better terms. But too much had happened. Too much trust had been broken.

"Can I call someone for you?" I asked.

"My mom is coming over."

"Okay." I put my hand on her shoulder for a squeeze, then stood. "Hope you feel better."

Katy was exactly where I'd expected when I passed the curtain, her ear all but pressed to the fabric. So I held out a hand, taking hers, then got us the hell out of the ER and went home.

"You want lunch?" I asked.

"I'm not really hungry. I kind of just want to play in my room."

"We'll eat in an hour or so."

"'Kay." She turned, about to head upstairs, but stopped. "Thanks for coming to get me."

"I'll always come to get you."

"I know."

I waited until she was upstairs, until I heard the click of her door close, to pull the phone from my pocket. I headed out back as I called Della, just to hear her voice.

"Hey." She sounded like she'd been crying.

Not the voice I'd hoped for. "What's wrong?"

"Luka." She blew out a long, frustrated breath. "He told me it was a dangerous game screwing a student's father."

"What? How would he even know?"

"He doesn't. He just thinks he does. And he's right, not that I'm going to tell him he's right, so I ignored him. But . . ."

"But he suspects something." And that was a huge damn problem. If Luka had some warped sense of possession over Della, if his ego had been bruised because she'd moved on, no way he'd keep our relationship a secret. "Fuck."

"Yep. Fuck." Hearing her say fuck would have been adorable if not for that wobble in her voice. "He's right."

No. My stomach dropped. "Della—"

"What are we doing? What am I doing?"

I walked across the yard to the firepit, sitting on the stack of bricks that still needed to be laid. "What do you want to do?"

"I'm Katy's teacher. This is my job. I thought maybe we could keep this a secret, but Jeff, if someone finds out . . ."

"So we wait." That was the only option.

"I'd understand if you didn't want to. If that's asking too much. We hardly know each other."

"It's not too much." Maybe her roommate couldn't go two months without a woman, but that dumb motherfucker had been blind to the treasure in front of him all along. For her, I'd wait without question. "It's only two months."

Two miserable months without her. Maybe I'd finish the garage. Maybe I'd finish this yard. Maybe I'd do everything around here I'd been putting off, so that in two months, she'd have my undivided attention.

God, what a fucking bad day.

"How are you?" she asked.

"I'm good," I lied. "But I'll let you go."

"Will you call me?" she asked.

Yeah, I'd call her. "Every day."

eleven
Della

When my phone rang, I scrambled to answer. "Well?"

"Signed," Jeff said. "Alcott is officially mine."

"Yes." I fist-pumped and giggled, excitement driving me out of my chair. "I'm so happy for you."

"Me too, baby. I'm nervous but . . . I still can't believe this is happening."

"You're going to do great," I said.

"Hope so."

"Know so."

It had been two months since I'd seen Jeff in person. Two agonizing months.

But true to his word, we'd talked every day. Usually it was at night. We'd FaceTime and talk for hours.

We talked about Rosalie. About how her trip to the ER last week had been eerily similar to a visit two months ago. She'd taken Katy along and Jeff had needed to go rescue her. And like months ago, the doctors hadn't found anything wrong.

Part of me kept expecting the doctors to uncover this mysterious illness. Each time she was sick, I'd get drawn in, waiting for the outcome. And each time Rosalie turned out to be fine, I felt a little bit like a chump.

The ER trips didn't seem to faze Jeff, other than hating when Katy was dragged along. Probably because he'd grown numb to Rosalie's manipulations.

Beyond that topic, we talked about anything. Everything.

I told him about my family. He told me about his. I could say with confidence I knew his favorite foods and candy, even if we hadn't shared them together.

And we talked about Hans and his retirement plan. How instead of waiting for the end of this season, Hans had decided to escalate the transition. He hadn't just accepted the idea of retirement but had embraced it.

Jeff would pay him over the next fifteen years per their contract, signed today, but he was the new official owner of Alcott Landscaping.

And tonight, we'd get to celebrate. Together.

"Three hours," he said.

I glanced at the clock. "Three hours."

Jitters danced through my limbs as I walked around my classroom, taking in the empty desks. It was the last day of school and the kids were already outside, loading into buses and cars on their way to summer break.

Katy was no longer my student, and she was staying at Rosalie's until Sunday. Staff members were expected to stay until four, but then I'd be going straight to Jeff's house to pick up where we'd left off two months ago.

"I'm nervous."

Jeff chuckled. "Why?"

"What if you don't like me anymore?"

"Della."

"I'm serious. What if it's different? What if the chemistry is gone?"

"Were you not paying attention last night? I came all over my stomach watching you finger that pretty pussy."

My cheeks flamed and I closed my eyes, picturing the way he'd looked last night. Before Jeff, I hadn't tried phone sex. Two months of watching through a screen as he'd stroke his cock had been the most excruciating type of foreplay.

"Don't be nervous," he murmured.

"Okay."

"Did you pack a bag?"

"Yep."

"Good. You're not leaving my house until Monday morning. I've missed you."

"I missed you too," I whispered. More than he'd ever know.

But maybe these past two months had been good for us. We'd had to set the physical connection aside, and though we'd mastered phone sex, most of our conversations were exactly that.

We'd shared our lives in the past two months through calls and texts.

Was it possible to make a best friend in two months? Was it possible to fall in love with a man in that time? I wouldn't have thought so before, but now . . .

"I'd better go," he said. "I've got some stuff to do before I take off. Three hours?"

"Three hours." Not a minute more. "Bye."

With the call ended, I went to my desk, grabbing the totes I'd brought along this morning. Teachers would be in the building for another two weeks before our summer break started, but I'd decided to pack up my desk today, taking home the gifts from students that I'd collected this year and the extras I'd kept on hand, like a box of tampons and a pair of gloves.

I was just starting to empty my bottom drawer when footsteps echoed in the hallway. Beyond my open door, Luka passed by.

He didn't stop.

I didn't wave.

The friendship we'd had for years was all but over. That morning when I'd come home from Jeff's house and Luka had made his snide comments about me sleeping with a parent, well . . . we were done.

Whatever suspicions he had, I'd refused to acknowledge. Instead, I'd spent a lot of time in my room with the door closed, either talking to Jeff or searching for apartments.

He must have expected it because when I'd told him this morning that I'd be leaving in September when my lease agreement ended, he hadn't at all been shocked.

Packing my desk would be a breeze compared to the house, but Jeff would help.

I was just finishing with a drawer when more footsteps sounded in the hallway. This time, they carried a visitor straight into the classroom.

"Rosalie?" I looked past her for Katy but she was alone. "Um, hi. Is everything okay?"

"Okay? No, it's not okay." Her lip curled. "I came to pick up Katy. You know, I almost left. I almost let this go. But I can't walk away. It's not right, what you did. Do you sleep with all your students' fathers? Or just my daughter's?"

My stomach dropped along with my jaw.

Somehow, she'd found out. Somehow, this secret hadn't been a secret. And maybe two months away from Jeff had been the solution, but we'd still crossed a line in the first place.

"Shame on you." Rosalie huffed, giving me a glare. Then

she turned and stormed out of my classroom as quickly as she'd entered.

"Oh God." I wrapped my hands around my stomach, feeling like I was going to hurl.

It wasn't like this had been some flimsy affair. It wasn't like he was still married to her. But the guilt, the shame, crept beneath my skin like a fog, gray and thick.

Jeff. I had to tell Jeff.

I spun for my desk where I'd left my phone, but before I could pick it up, another voice filled the room.

"I knew it." Luka scoffed. "I'll give you credit though. You hid it well. I was starting to second-guess myself. Do you guys meet to fuck when you say you're going to the grocery store? Or maybe a quickie before work?"

Once upon a time, I'd loved this man. Or . . . I'd thought I loved him.

I faced him, squaring my shoulders. Then I said something that was long, long overdue. "Fuck you, Luka. Why does this bother you? Because I'm not dangling on your chain anymore?"

He had to have known about my crush. And he'd exploited it. He'd kept me in his life for when it was convenient for him. For the nights when he was alone and needed a companion.

"You're the one fucking a student's father, Della."

And my indiscretion would give him a reason to blame this all on me. To turn me into the villain.

Maybe I was.

He looked me up and down, shaking his head. "What happened to you?"

Jeff Dawson. He'd turned my life upside down. Or maybe he'd turned it right-side up.

"I met someone worthy." I crossed the room, passing him for the door. "And I made a mistake."

A mistake I intended to own.

So I kept my chin up as I walked to the principal's office.

twelve

Jeff

One hour.

Just one more hour and this hiatus from Della would be over.

The texts, the calls, just hadn't been enough. I missed her eyes. I missed touching her hair. I missed her in my bed.

One hour to go. Then she was mine.

Since I'd spoken to her earlier, time had slowed to a goddamn crawl. Every three minutes I checked the clock. I'd attempted to busy myself with work, answering emails and returning calls, but I was too keyed up to focus.

"Hey, boss." Korbyn smirked as he passed by my open doorway.

That smirk was because he was the only other person at Alcott who knew I'd signed papers with Hans today.

Monday, Hans and I would make the official announcement to the staff, but I'd asked him to keep it quiet until next week. Tonight, I wanted to celebrate with Della. I wanted to tell Katy on Sunday after I picked her up from Rosalie's. For the weekend, I wanted this to be my quiet victory.

Come Monday, I'd step into Hans's shoes. Hopefully, I'd

be able to fill them. And the shoes Finn Alcott had left years ago.

Would Finn care that I'd be running his former business?

A week ago, Della and I had been talking about The Maysen Jar. How she'd discovered it in college. I'd had no idea that Finn's sister owned that restaurant. Maybe, with any luck, I'd bump into him. I could tell him myself that his namesake was under my charge.

That I'd work my ass off to make this a success.

I could do this, right? *I could do this.*

When Hans had approached me about escalating our timeline, I'd almost told him no, to wait until the fall. But it had been Della's confidence that had made me agree. Her faith in me was humbling.

I could do this.

There was a mountain of things to worry about, but I was setting it aside until Monday.

My phone rang on my desk, Katy's name on the screen. "Hey, Dandelion. How was the last day of school?"

"Daddy." Her voice cracked and, with it, my heart.

I was out of my chair in a flash, searching for my truck keys. "What's wrong?"

"Mom r-read my diary."

"Oh." I sank into my chair. Not an emergency. It would be for a twelve-year-old, but not one that meant I was racing across town. I dragged a hand through my hair, my heart climbing out of my throat. "Well, that's not good."

She sniffled and then the sobbing began.

"Take a deep breath." My poor girl. It hurt hearing her cry when I couldn't pull her into a hug. "It will be okay."

"N-no, it won't. She went into the school."

"Okay," I drawled, my spine stiffening. "What was in your diary?"

"I-I saw you."

"You saw me."

"And M-miss Adler."

Oh. Fuck. I shot out of the chair again, snagging my keys and bolting for the door. "What did you write, Katy? Be specific."

"S-sorry." She sobbed harder.

"It's okay." Like hell was this okay, but I kept my voice gentle despite my panic. I started jogging down the hall, heading straight for the doors and my truck parked outside. "What was in your diary?"

"It was that weekend that she played games with us. I woke up early and snuck downstairs when I heard you talking. You were at the door and kissed her."

Yep. We were fucked.

Shit. If Della lost her job . . . I'd never forgive myself.

I climbed in the truck, the phone still pressed to my ear as I reversed out of my space and tore down the lane toward town. "What did your mother do?"

"I don't know." Katy hiccupped. "She told me to stay in the car and she went inside. Then she came out and was mad on the drive home. When I got here, she had my diary on the table."

Damn it, Rosalie.

"I'm sorry," Katy cried.

"It's not your fault. It's mine." I should have talked to her about Della. I should have trusted her with the truth. "Was there anything else in the diary?"

"I wrote some not nice things about Hailee."

"That's it?" No crush on a boy? No smoking? No drinking?

"And I, um . . ." Her voice quieted. "I wrote some bad stuff about Mom. How she isn't really sick, she just wants

your attention and how selfish she can be and how sometimes she says mean stuff about you and it's not true and she
knows it's not true but she says it anyway when she knows it
bothers me because I don't like when she says mean things
about you."

I sighed. What a cluster. "I love you, Katy. I don't care if
your mom says mean stuff about me."

"You don't say mean stuff about her."

No, I didn't. Not anymore. "It doesn't matter. All that
matters is you."

She sniffled and another sob choked loose. "I'm really
sorry, Daddy. Will you talk to Miss Adler?"

"Yeah, I'll talk to her. We'll figure this out." I made it a
point not to lie to my daughter, but today, she needed that lie.
"What are you doing right now?"

"Sitting in my room. Mom took my phone."

"So how are you calling me?"

"My watch."

"Ah." I nodded, hitting the turn signal as I raced through
town.

"I'm grounded," she muttered, a flare of anger breaking
past the sadness in her little voice. "I wish it was Sunday."

"I wish it was Sunday too." Then Katy would be at my
house where she belonged. "Just hang tight."

"Okay." She blew out a long breath. "This is going to
suck."

"Probably."

"Are you going to see Miss Adler right now?"

"Yep."

"Will you tell her I'm sorry?"

I loved this girl's heart. "Yeah, I'll tell her."

"Thanks. I'd better go," Katy whispered. "I can hear
Mom."

In another situation, I might have encouraged Katy to make amends. To talk to her mother. But not today.

Rosalie had a right to be hurt. Whatever Katy wrote was probably ruthless. But instead of taking a look in the mirror, instead of realizing that our daughter had a point, she'd taken it out on Della.

So as far as I was concerned, Rosalie could fuck off.

"Bye," I said, ending the call. Then I focused on the road, getting to the school and parking in the drop-off loop.

The building was quiet, relaxed, like it had let out a sigh having made it through the end of another year. My boots thudded on the floor as I strode to Della's classroom.

She was sitting at her desk. There were two tote bags on top, each full of stuff she'd probably taken from her desk.

"Hey."

She blinked, her eyes glassy as she spun her chair my direction. Then her chin started to quiver as she stood, waiting for me to wrap her up.

That was exactly what I did.

I breathed her in, holding her tight as she sank into my chest. "I'm sorry, beautiful. I'm so sorry."

"I missed your smell." Her arms snaked around my waist, banding tight.

"What happened?"

"Rosalie is kind of a bitch."

I barked a laugh. "I'm aware."

"But she didn't tell my boss."

"She didn't?" I let her go. Okay, maybe I wasn't as pissed at Rosalie as I had been a minute ago.

"No." Della gave me a sad smile. "But I did."

Because she was the type of woman who admitted a mistake. It was one of many things I'd learned about her through those phone calls and texts over the past two months. Down to her core, Della Adler was pure light. A goodness unparalleled.

Probably why I'd fallen for her so quickly.

"Did you get fired?"

"No." Her shoulders sagged. "Thank God. My principal said that because I've never had another incident that she'd only give me a warning and an official reprimand in my file. I promised her that we hit the brakes and haven't seen each other while we were waiting for the end of the year and I think she believed me. But Jeff, it was so humiliating. I hate getting in trouble."

"But you didn't lose your job."

She shook her head. "I didn't lose my job."

"Thank fuck." I hauled her into my chest again, burying my nose in her hair. "I'm sorry."

"It's okay. I knew it was a risk." She buried her nose in my shirt, her voice muffled. "How did Rosalie even find out?"

"Katy. She saw us one morning. Wrote about it in her diary."

Della gasped, leaning back. "And Rosalie read her diary? That is sacred."

"Sacred?"

"To a twelve-year-old girl? Absolutely."

"So you're saying I shouldn't read Katy's diary," I teased.

"Don't even joke about that." She pointed at my nose as I fought a grin.

Damn, but she was beautiful. "Fuck, but I missed you."

I framed her face with my hands and crushed my mouth to hers, sliding past those soft lips for the taste I'd been craving for months.

A whimper escaped her throat as she melted, our tongues tangling. It was too short, too timid, for how I wanted to kiss her, but before I hiked up the hem of her dress and fucked her on her desk—that would definitely get her fired—I pulled away and nodded to the totes.

"Saw those and thought you were packing up your desk."

"Well, I am. That's everything I don't want to leave here this summer."

"Ah."

Della had a lot of packing in her future. She'd promised to tell that dumb fuck roommate of hers she was leaving this morning.

Not that I wanted her living with him, but if I was lucky, I'd get her to the point where she was spending day and night at my house. Then maybe she'd realize there was no reason for her to rent a house on her own come September.

Not when she belonged in mine.

There wasn't a doubt in my mind that we'd make it. Something with Della had always felt right. Felt steady. But I'd give her time to catch up.

"How long do you need to stay?" I asked.

She glanced over her shoulder at the clock. "It's probably close enough. I'm ready to get out of here."

I took the totes, looping them over a forearm, then with my free hand, I clasped hers, leading her out of the classroom. We'd just stepped into the hallway when Della stopped.

Three doors down, Luka stood outside his own classroom.

So I lifted Della's clasped hand to my lips, kissing her knuckles. Then I gave her a tug, leading her in the opposite direction.

She giggled. "I told him to fuck off today."

"How'd that feel?"

"Good." She smiled up at me, those caramel eyes dancing. "I wish we didn't have to wait until Sunday to get Katy."

That. Right there. That was why I'd fallen in love with Della.

We walked outside and to my truck. The Jeep could stay at the school until tomorrow. And instead of taking her to my house, I drove the opposite direction.

"Where are we going?" she asked.

"Hungry?"

"Yes. How'd you know?"

Because I knew Della. In the past two months, I needed both hands and a foot to count the number of times she'd forgotten to eat lunch because she'd been wrapped up with a student or an assignment. Given today's situation, not a chance she'd remembered lunch.

"Lucky guess." I gave her a wink, then I drove us to The Maysen Jar.

That was the day I took the love of my life on our first date.

epilogue
Jeff

E*leven years later . . .*
  "Junebug," I called from the base of the stairs. "We're late."

"I'm coming, Daddy!" Harper yelled.

That was the third time she'd said she was coming. "Two minutes."

"I'm hurrying." The thud of her footsteps pounded on the floor as she raced from one room to the other.

I sighed, checking my watch. I couldn't remember a time when I wasn't waiting on a daughter or my wife.

Not a bad way for a man to spend his life. Even if that meant we were always running behind.

"Carter, are you ready?" I asked.

"Yep." He rounded the corner from the dining room wearing his coat and his backpack. Knowing my son, he'd been ready for ten minutes.

When it came to being on time, Carter was my only hope. He was the most responsible, organized seven-year-old I'd ever known.

"Do you have your lunch box?" he asked.

"Shouldn't I be asking you that question?" I bent to give him a hug.

"Do you?" He smiled up at me, revealing the gap between his front teeth that would one day see braces.

"Yes, I have my lunch. It's already in the truck." I touched the tip of his nose. "Love you, bud."

"Love you too."

I smoothed his hair, the same shade as mine. Everyone always said that Carter resembled me, but when I looked at him, I saw Della. The same was true with Harper. Though not many disagreed when it came to our daughter. Harper looked more and more like Della every day.

"One minute," I hollered up to her.

"I'm almost ready!" Harper was nine, almost ten, and it felt too soon for us to be at this stage. According to Della, she was a budding fashionista, always worried about her clothes or headbands or shoes.

"She's never ready." Carter blew out a long breath, leaning against my leg. "We're going to be late."

"You'll make it." I leaned down to kiss his cheek, then swatted his backpack. "Go load up in the car. They'll be right behind you."

"Okay."

"Have a good day at school."

"Bye." He rushed down the hall, his backpack bouncing as he made his way to the garage.

A few years ago, we'd connected the house to the garage so Della wouldn't have to traipse in and out with the kids. The minute the door closed behind him, I clapped. "Time's up, Junebug. We're out the door."

"Two seconds!"

I tipped my head to the ceiling and let out a groan.

Della's laugh drifted from the hallway. She walked my

way carrying a travel mug of coffee in one hand with her own backpack slung over a shoulder. "We're late."

"Yep."

"One day, I want to be early."

I chuckled, pulling her into my arms. "You and me both, baby."

"It's probably overrated."

"We'll never know." I dropped a kiss to her mouth, taking in today's outfit.

Black jeans. Oversized sweater. Earrings so long they nearly brushed her shoulders. There was a reason Harper loved clothes. Because her mother loved clothes.

Instead of connecting the garage to the house, we should have built another closet.

But it was Della's sparkling caramel eyes that took my breath away. "You look beautiful. I'm already looking forward to stripping that sweater off you later."

"Tease." She kissed the underside of my jaw. "Love you."

"I love you too." I kissed her again, lingering a bit to stroke my tongue against hers.

"I'm ready." Harper's voice broke us apart as she tore down the stairs. Her hair was up in a knot like Della's.

"That's not the outfit we laid out last night," Della said, looking her up and down.

"I changed my mind."

Just once, I wanted her to wear the clothes we insisted she set out the night before. "Carter's in the car. Get going."

"Bye, Daddy." Harper gave me a quick hug and a kiss on the cheek as I helped her into her coat and handed over her backpack.

"Have a good day." Della kissed me again.

"You too." I followed them to the garage, making sure they were in. Then I breathed a sigh and checked the time.

Yep, they were late.

But Della wouldn't drive fast to make up time, not with our babies in the car. She'd drop them at the elementary school, then get to the middle school, probably walking in the door the second the bell rang.

Thankfully, she'd taken her first period as prep this year so she didn't have to worry.

She was still at the same school, teaching middle schoolers. That black mark on her record, earned by our relationship, never had amounted to much, not when we'd gotten married that next fall.

It had only taken a month for me to convince Della to move in. She'd left that house with Luka and never looked back—that idiot had changed schools the next year and neither of us had been sad to see him disappear.

A month after she'd moved in, we'd become engaged. Rosalie had given me an earful about rushing into a relationship with Katy's teacher, to which I'd told her to mind her own fucking business.

Then three months later, surrounded by our family and closest friends, we'd gotten married in the backyard. Della had wanted a winter wonderland for the ceremony. Mother Nature had dumped six inches of snow two days before the wedding so she'd gotten her wish.

Harper was born that next June, and I'd been calling her Junebug ever since.

I was headed for the kitchen to grab my own travel mug of coffee for the drive to the office when my phone vibrated in my pocket. Someone must have forgotten something. I expected Della's name on the screen but it was Katy's. "Hi, Dandelion."

"Hi, Dad. I'm running late."

"Your outfit? Because that was your sister's struggle this morning."

"No." She laughed. "I'm dressed. But I was trying to find some old pictures. I had this idea for the Michaelson project, and I was thinking about that trip we took to Oregon my sophomore year. What was the name of that hotel?"

"The Gallaway."

"That's it. They had the prettiest flower beds. I was hoping to use it for inspiration, but I can't find any pictures from that trip in the photo books Della made me."

From the day we'd gotten together, Della had made it her mission to document Katy's life. Every year, she put together a photo book. She'd been doing the same for Harper and Carter since they were born.

She'd print two copies, one for us. One for the kids.

When Katy had moved into her own house last year, Della had taken over her books, but maybe she'd missed one.

"I can check in the shed," I told her.

"Okay, thanks. I'm leaving now so I'll see you at the office. Be warned, I got so distracted by this I didn't pack a lunch."

"Then I guess we'd better plan to go out to lunch. The Maysen Jar?"

"Where else?"

That little restaurant hadn't changed much over the past decade. Not that it needed to. It had a timeless charm and no matter how often we ate there, we kept going back.

"All right," I said. "See you in a bit."

Katy had turned twenty-three this month. After graduating from Montana State with her degree, she'd decided to come work at Alcott. Originally, she'd planned to help me run the business side of things, but lately, she'd taken an interest in the actual landscape design.

Maybe it was all those years she'd tagged along with me on jobs.

Whatever the reason, I was more than happy to have her riding shotgun in my truck. Her, and the dog.

She and Della eventually wore me down and we adopted a puppy after Harper was born. A golden retriever named Ollie. He'd always been Katy's dog, even when she hadn't lived in our house. So when she'd finally gotten a place of her own, the dog had moved out. But since Katy was never far from Ollie, the back of my truck was covered in his blond hair.

Della had made a few comments lately about another dog for Harper and Carter. This time, I wanted a dog that didn't shed so damn much. Maybe a dog, like Ollie, who'd tag along at work too.

It had been a successful decade for Alcott Landscaping. Hans had been happily retired, traveling the world with his wife, while I ran the business. The last five years had been so profitable that I'd nearly paid off my contract.

My goal was to own it free and clear sooner rather than later. And someday, if my kids wanted to take over, it would be the legacy Della and I could give them.

With my coffee and keys, I headed to the yard, walking beneath the light strings. Every night, Della turned them on so that their golden glow shined through the house's windows, even in the dead of winter.

This space had become the signpost for important events in our lives. Birthday parties. Katy's high school graduation. Baby showers. Della and I had talked about moving to a bigger house, especially during those years when we had three kids under our roof. But in the end, we'd decided to stay. Mostly because we didn't want to leave this yard.

Instead, we'd found little ways to expand storage, like the

shed we'd built onto the back side of the garage. I unlocked the door, then ducked inside and flipped on the light. The far wall was lined with storage totes, so I set my cup aside and started digging.

The first three tubs I pulled down were full of Christmas decorations. The fourth was full of Katy's stuff from her childhood bedroom.

I dug through the jerseys and art projects and mementos, feeling a book at the bottom, so I tugged it free.

A diary.

"I remember you." I chuckled, inspecting the dandelion diary I'd given her ages ago. The diary that had caused so much drama. I thumbed through the pages, my heart squeezing at the young, blocky handwriting inside. Katy didn't write like that anymore.

Della would kick my ass for even touching this book, but I thumbed to the first entry.

Dear Diary,

My dad needs a girlfriend, and I've already picked her out.

"What the fuck?" My jaw dropped as I continued to read, entry after entry. By the time I was done, my head was spinning.

She'd set us up. A twelve-year-old kid had entirely manipulated her grown-ass father.

From that first day when she'd gotten in trouble for cussing, to the day she'd cried in class. Even to that last day when Rosalie had found her diary.

Not this diary.

According to this one, Katy had planted a fake diary, knowing Rosalie would read it. She'd counted on her mother making a scene. Hoping it would bring Della and me together.

Katy hadn't realized that Della and I weren't broken up. We'd just been waiting for the end of the school year.

"I'll be damned."

Manipulated by my own flesh and blood.

A laugh bubbled free, followed by another until I was roaring, my hand on my belly because it hurt to laugh so hard.

It took a few minutes to pull myself together. I returned that diary to the bottom of the tub, closing the lid, then found the photo book Katy wanted.

With it tucked beneath my arm, I locked the shed and headed to work.

"Morning, Dad." Katy smiled as I strode into her office.

"I love you." I rounded her desk, dropping a kiss to her hair.

"Love you too."

With a wink, I retreated to my own office and sent Della a text.

Remember that diary Katy used to write in all the time?

Her reply was instant. *The dandelion diary?*

the dandelion diary

Dear Diary,

My plan is brilliant! Miss Adler came to the pizza place tonight and she totally has a crush on Dad. She even came over for game night. He couldn't stop staring at her, and I think they were like touching feet or something beneath the table. I don't really know what that means but I'm guessing it's love.

Katy

Hey Diary,

It worked! So easy!!! Dad and Miss Adler are together. Like, together together. I woke up early this morning and heard noises so I snuck down a few stairs. They were whispering and touching and then he kissed her. She slept over! I know what that means. The girls in eighth grade were talking about sex in the bathroom one day. (Eww.) Anyway, this is the best day ever! Do you think they'll have kids when they get married? I really want a brother or sister. Okay, it's really early and I'm really tired so I'm going back to bed.

Katy

———————

Dear Diary,

My plan is falling apart. It was going perfectly and now it's all wrecked. They messed it up. Miss Adler hasn't been here in weeks. Every time I bring up her name to Dad, he changes the subject. Do they not like each other anymore? I just don't understand. They like each other. I just know it. When they're together, I can tell. They smile a lot and always sneak looks at each other. What happened? They need to see each other again. Be together, and then they'll remember. I think I need to do something big. Time for a new plan.

Katy

———————

Diary,

Okay, here's what I'm going to do. I bought another diary at the book fair yesterday. It's going to be my fake. I'll write a bunch of stuff in it and then leave it out at Mom's. She'll read it for sure. She doesn't even kind of care that it's private.

I think that if I write some stuff about Miss Adler, she'll say something to Dad. Mom doesn't even know what mind her own business means. I'm counting on her being her. Whatever she says, it will mean that Dad and Miss Adler will probably have to talk. I just need them to talk.

Tomorrow is the last day of school and this is my only hope. If they go the whole summer without seeing each other, they'll never get together. What if she starts dating someone else and doesn't even know that she was meant to be with Dad? I can't let that happen.

Wish me luck. Oh, and I'm sure Mom will ground me forever too. Yay me.
Katy

Dear Diary,

It worked! Dad and Miss Adler are dating! They came to get me from Mom's today and we went to dinner and they held hands the whole entire time. I think they might even be in love? I can't believe this is happening. Like I hoped it would work but I wasn't really sure. Mom is still super mad. Worth it. My plan worked! Miss Adler told me before bed I could start calling her Della now that she's Dad's girlfriend. SHE'S HIS GIRLFRIEND! I wonder if she'd help me convince him to get a puppy? I like the name Daisy for a girl and Ollie for a boy.

Katy

acknowledgments

Thank you for reading *The Dandelion Diary*! This was such a lovely story to add to a beloved series. I smiled every day writing Jeff and Della's book. I hope you smiled while reading it too. Special thanks to my editor, Elizabeth Nover, and my proofreaders, Julie Deaton and Judy Zweifel. And thank you to Liz, Jillian and MJ for inviting me into the 1001 Dark Nights family!

about the author

Devney Perry is a *Wall Street Journal* and *USA Today* bestselling author of over forty romance novels. After working in the technology industry for a decade, she abandoned conference calls and project schedules to pursue her passion for writing. She was born and raised in Montana and now lives in Washington with her husband and two sons.

Don't miss out on Devney's latest book news.
Subscribe to her newsletter!
www.devneyperry.com

1001 dark nights

Sign up for the 1001 Dark Nights Newsletter and be entered to win a Tiffany Key necklace.

There's a contest every month!

Go to www.1001DarkNights.com to subscribe.

As a bonus, all subscribers can download FIVE FREE exclusive books!

discover 1001 dark nights collection ten

DRAGON LOVER by Donna Grant
A Dragon Kings Novella

KEEPING YOU by Aurora Rose Reynolds
An Until Him/Her Novella

HAPPILY EVER NEVER by Carrie Ann Ryan
A Montgomery Ink Legacy Novella

DESTINED FOR ME by Corinne Michaels
A Come Back for Me/Say You'll Stay Crossover

MADAM ALANA by Audrey Carlan
A Marriage Auction Novella

DIRTY FILTHY BILLIONAIRE by Laurelin Paige
A Dirty Universe Novella

HIDE AND SEEK by Laura Kaye
A Blasphemy Novella

TANGLED WITH YOU by J. Kenner
A Stark Security Novella

TEMPTED by Lexi Blake
A Masters and Mercenaries Novella

THE DANDELION DIARY by Devney Perry
A Maysen Jar Novella

CHERRY LANE by Kristen Proby
A Huckleberry Bay Novella

THE GRAVE ROBBER by Darynda Jones
A Charley Davidson Novella

CRY OF THE BANSHEE by Heather Graham
A Krewe of Hunters Novella

DARKEST NEED by Rachel Van Dyken
A Dark Ones Novella

CHRISTMAS IN CAPE MAY by Jennifer Probst
A Sunshine Sisters Novella

A VAMPIRE'S MATE by Rebecca Zanetti
A Dark Protectors/Rebels Novella

WHERE IT BEGINS by Helena Hunting
A Pucked Novella

also from blue box press

THE MARRIAGE AUCTION by Audrey Carlan
Season One, Volume One
Season One, Volume Two
Season One, Volume Three
Season One, Volume Four

SAPPHIRE STORM by Christopher Rice writing as C.
Travis Rice
A Sapphire Cove Novel

ATLAS: THE STORY OF PA SALT by Lucinda Riley and
Harry Whittaker

A SOUL OF ASH AND BLOOD by Jennifer L. Armentrout
A Blood and Ash Novel

START US UP by Lexi Blake
A Park Avenue Promise Novel

THE JEWELER OF STOLEN DREAMS by M.J. Rose

LOVE ON THE BYLINE by Xio Axelrod
A Plays and Players Novel

FIGHTING THE PULL by Kristen Ashley
A River Rain Novel

A FIRE IN THE FLESH by Jennifer L. Armentrout
FLAME by Jennifer L.

on behalf of 1001 dark nights

Liz Berry, M.J. Rose, and Jillian Stein would like to thank ~

Steve Berry
Doug Scofield
Benjamin Stein
Kim Guidroz
Tanaka Kangara
Asha Hossain
Chris Graham
Chelle Olson
Kasi Alexander
Jessica Saunders
Stacey Tardif
Dylan Stockton
Kate Boggs
Richard Blake
and Simon Lipskar

Printed in Great Britain
by Amazon

34910478R00098